"I know what you are thinking," he said, his voice soft and sensual—and closer than she expected.

Her eyes popped open to find him hovering over her. She stopped swaying and gazed up at him. How could any one man be so attractive? He was like a fallen angel with his dark hair and mesmerizing stare.

"No, you don't," she replied, her heart thrumming in her breast.

He slipped an arm around her, hauled her closer. "I am thinking of it too."

Her brain sent the signal to back away, but too late. His other hand grasped one of hers, placed it on the hard muscle of his biceps. Another pull and she was flush against his body.

Breast to belly to hip. His arousal came as a surprise, and her breath broke on a gasp.

"Yes, I want you," he said.

"But you hate me."

His easy grin had the power to light the dark corners of her soul. He was so much like the old Alejandro in that moment that it made her ache.

"And you hate me. This does not stop our bodies from desiring one another, *si?*"

Dear Reader,

Romance novels change lives. The first romances I ever read were about handsome tycoons and independent women, exotic locations and passion so intense it made my heart pound as I raced to the end of the book. I loved those stories, and I often dreamed of writing one of my own.

But I never sat down to try until a friend sent me a contest announcement. The editors at Harlequin Presents were looking for new writers and had decided to hold a writing competition.

I sat at my computer and a man appeared. A gorgeous, arrogant Spaniard named Alejandro. And he wasn't very happy. When Rebecca Layton arrived, I realized what was wrong. Rebecca and Alejandro had a very emotional past—and their futures were about to collide as Alejandro set into motion a plan for revenge.

I e-mailed my entry only hours before the deadline. A month later, I got the call that I'd won the Harlequin Presents® Instant Seduction contest. I was stunned—and ecstatic. Now, during Harlequin's sixtieth anniversary year, I am so happy to be a new author and to share Alejandro and Rebecca's story with you. I hope it makes your heart pound, and I hope you race to the end of the book to find out what happens.

Please visit me at www.lynnrayeharris.com. I would love to hear what you think about my Spanish magnate and his red-hot revenge.

Happy reading,

Lynn Raye Harris

Lynn Raye Harris
SPANISH MAGNATE, RED-HOT REVENGE

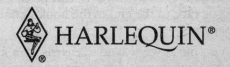

HARLEQUIN®

TORONTO • NEW YORK • LONDON
AMSTERDAM • PARIS • SYDNEY • HAMBURG
STOCKHOLM • ATHENS • TOKYO • MILAN • MADRID
PRAGUE • WARSAW • BUDAPEST • AUCKLAND

Recycling programs
for this product may
not exist in your area.

ISBN-13: 978-0-373-12848-8

SPANISH MAGNATE, RED-HOT REVENGE

First North American Publication 2009.

www.eHarlequin.com

Printed in U.S.A.

All about the author...
Lynn Raye Harris

LYNN RAYE HARRIS read her first Harlequin
romance when her grandmother carted home a
box from a yard sale. She didn't know she wanted
to be a writer then, but she definitely knew she
wanted to marry a sheikh or a prince and live the
glamorous life she read about in the pages. Instead
she married a military man and moved around the
world. She's been inside the Kremlin, hiked up a
Korean mountain, floated on a gondola in Venice
and stood inside volcanoes at opposite ends of the
world.

These days Lynn lives in North Alabama with her
handsome husband and two crazy cats. When
she's not writing, she loves to read, shop for
antiques, cook gourmet meals and try new wines.
She is also an avowed shoeaholic and thinks
there's nothing better than a new pair of high
heels.

Lynn was a finalist in the 2008 Romance Writers
of America Golden Heart® contest, and she is
the winner of the Harlequin Presents Instant
Seduction contest. She loves a hot hero,
a heroine with attitude and a happy ending.
Writing passionate stories for Harlequin is
a dream come true. You can visit Lynn at
www.lynnrayeharris.com.

To my husband, Mike, who bought me my first
computer and who always believed.

Thanks for putting up with takeout, frozen dinners
and no dinners. You are my hero.

CHAPTER ONE

"THIS can't be happening," Rebecca Layton murmured.

She lifted her stunned gaze to the floor-to-ceiling picture window fronting her Waikiki suite. Of all the times to be away from New York. Palms swayed in the tropical trade winds, danced rhythmically against white-capped turquoise waves. So beautiful and peaceful. A stark contrast to the turmoil raging inside her.

She'd just gotten off the phone with Layton International's chief financial officer. The news wasn't good. If she didn't get back to New York and take control of the situation she could lose everything. Her cell phone rang again and she automatically picked it up. Very few people had her private number, and even fewer would dare disturb her when she was on a business trip.

Unless it was important. And right now Layton International's vulnerability was nothing short of cataclysmic.

"Yes?" she said as she reached for her planner. She could at least make a few calls while her executive assistant booked their return flight. She would *not* lose this company her family had built, in spite of the problems her father had left her with when he had died unexpectedly. He'd trusted her to take care of things. She would not fail him.

"Hello, Rebecca."

Rebecca's breath sliced into her lungs as her head whipped up. The planner slid from her lap. "Alejandro?"

"You did not expect to hear from me again, *no*?"

Rebecca closed her eyes, her gut clenching with a mixture of need and sorrow. Five long years since she'd heard that voice speak her name. Once he'd meant everything to her. Now?

Now she couldn't even begin to sort out how speaking to him made her feel. Sweat moistened her palms. "This is a bad time, Alejandro. I really can't talk."

His laugh, so cool and controlled, brought an image back to her. Alejandro Arroyo Rivera de Ramirez, the sexiest man she'd ever seen, naked to the waist, water streaming from his muscular chest in rivulets as he'd lifted himself from the pool. His sexy laugh as he'd scooped her up and hauled her into the bedroom. He hadn't even dried off. The second she'd said yes he'd come for her. And then he'd spent the night showing her how amazing he truly was.

"You need only listen, *querida*."

Something in his tone silenced her automatic protest.

Her heart kicked into double time. She reached for her forgotten wineglass, took a steadying sip.

"I expect you in Madrid in twenty-four hours. Spend the flight thinking how you will convince me to keep you on Layton International's board of directors."

Shock rocketed her to her feet. Her heart threatened to pound right out of her chest. "*You're* the one trying to steal my company?"

"You have made poor decisions, Rebecca. Do not continue to do so." His voice dripped ice.

Rebecca speared a hand through her hair as cold sweat spread over her skin. *Oh, God.* She wasn't the one who'd made poor decisions—but what did it matter now? Her father had thought he'd been doing the right thing.

They'd tumbled far in the five years since she'd last seen

Alejandro. Then, she'd been the one with the knowledge about the hotel business, the one with the might of a multi-million-dollar company behind her. He'd been the new kid on the block, the one with everything to learn.

How had everything changed so drastically?

There was still time. Not much, but a little. She could turn it around, could stop him. She *would* stop him, or she wasn't a Layton through and through. She forced herself to sound calm, controlled—though she was anything but. "It's not over yet. You're counting chickens."

"Counting chickens?" His laugh jarred her with its sudden warmth. "Ah, one of your Americanisms." She heard him speaking to someone in Spanish. "It is a done deal, Rebecca. Layton International belongs to Ramirez Enterprises."

She felt the chill of his words as if someone had picked her up and thrust her into the arctic. It was an odd sensation, totally at odds with her memory of the heat he'd once incited. She swallowed the knot in her throat. "I don't believe you."

"Then stay in Hawaii while I hire a new CEO. Or come advise the board on how to handle my new acquisition. Your choice."

He knew she was in Hawaii? Did he also know about the deal she'd just closed to acquire a chain of resorts in the islands?

The deal that would have saved everything in just a few short months. Rebecca sank onto a rattan chair as her legs refused to hold her up any longer. The certainty in his voice was undeniable.

She knew from personal experience how determined Alejandro could be when he wanted something. He didn't rest until he'd won, until he'd imposed his will and gotten exactly what he wanted. If he was calling her now, he was very certain he had control.

Lock, stock and barrel, as her dad would have said. Jackson Layton was probably spinning in his grave right this instant.

He'd never liked Alejandro, would be shattered to know the company he'd built had fallen into his enemy's hands. And all because his daughter hadn't seen it coming.

"I think I hate you," she said softly.

"Then we are even." The line went dead.

Rebecca leaned numbly against the soft leather seat of the Mercedes that had picked her up at the Madrid Barajas International Airport. She stared bleary-eyed at the scenery as the car carried her down the Gran Via.

He'd said he hated her. It shouldn't surprise her, but somehow it did.

Five long years. She hadn't seen him—other than glimpses on television or in the pages of a magazine—in all that time. For one month he'd been everything to her. He'd been there when she woke, when she fell asleep, when she swam or shopped or ate. He'd laughed and made love to her and made her think she was the most special woman in the world.

Now? She pinched the bridge of her nose. God only knew what happened now. He was ruthless, and he'd gained control of Layton International. He owned every last share. She'd confirmed it during her endless hours of travel.

She had nothing left. If he fired her, she could only limp away in shame. Without her company she was stone-cold broke. She could pay her mortgage for the next three months, and she could eat. If she hadn't found a job by then she'd lose her apartment and all her belongings.

Somehow the loss didn't compare to the loss of self-respect, the knowledge that she'd failed to protect her family legacy. She didn't know how to do anything except run a chain of hotels. It was what she'd been brought up to do—however reluctantly on her father's behalf—what she'd spent her life training for and trying to excel at. What would her father say if he could see her now? He'd wanted a son to leave the business to, but she was all he'd had. Would he now believe his concern about leaving a woman in charge was justified? She couldn't bear to think of his disappointment.

The car wound through the busy streets, nearing the ornate gray facade of the Villa de Musica, the Ramirez crown jewel in the heart of Madrid. Her heart hurt with the memories seeing it again brought. She'd been staying in the newly renovated hotel when she had first met Alejandro.

Rebecca shoved away thoughts of the sexy Spaniard who had ruined her life. She'd see him soon enough, and though her stomach twisted, she reminded herself—firmly—that she was here for business. She would not be intimidated. His mere presence wouldn't turn her to mush like it once had.

She was only mildly surprised when the car continued past the hotel. She hadn't really expected to be shown to a room, allowed to freshen up, maybe sleep a little, before being dragged into Alejandro's presence. Since she had no idea where they were going, she tried to close her eyes and get a few minutes' sleep—but rest eluded her.

Finally, after what seemed like hours in traffic, the limo pulled into a private drive somewhere in the hills of Madrid. She wasn't sure where they were, but she vaguely remembered passing the Palacio Real, the official residence of the King and Queen of Spain. A uniformed man helped her from the vehicle while another retrieved her bags. Within moments she was whisked through a stunning marble atrium and into a masculine office overlooking a terrace with a pool. How far Alejandro had come in five years.

Rebecca drifted over to the window and clasped her hands together. Oddly, they were shaking. But she'd been traveling for almost twenty-four hours straight. Her wrinkled suit clung to her body like an old rag, her curls had lost their bounce hours ago and she desperately needed a hot shower. Clearly

Alejandro would give her no quarter before he gloated over his triumph.

Well, fine. She'd endure it, and she'd refuse to react to his insults.

When the door behind her opened again, she put on her battle face and turned to meet him head-on.

And, oh heavens, he was still the most amazingly handsome man she'd ever met. Her knees threatened to buckle at the sight of him. She had an inexplicable urge to rush into his embrace, the way she used to do, but she crossed her arms and stood her ground. It took every ounce of reserve she had not to give in to the desire to touch him.

Why?

She didn't know if she was questioning her reaction or if the word was meant for him.

Why, Alejandro? Why did you deceive me when I loved you? Why have you done this to me now?

As if she'd spoken aloud, he halted, his gaze locking with hers. What lay behind those silver-gray eyes was anyone's guess, but she didn't think they held any warmth for her. And it hurt. Surprisingly, it hurt. She felt like she should do or say something, but she simply stood and drank him in.

If he'd changed at all, she couldn't see it. He was tall, six-three or six-four, and as muscular as ever. The years had not been unkind to him. He still looked every inch the hardened ex-bullfighter. She'd once teased him that he was a warrior clad in Armani.

Had she really spent hours exploring his tanned skin? It seemed so long ago that it must surely be her imagination. But she remembered with every last nerve-ending in her body how extraordinary it had felt when he slid his hard length inside her. Over and over and over, until she'd shuddered from the exquisite pleasure.

Rebecca pushed a hand against the stucco window casing

to steady herself. Alejandro didn't seem to notice. He was completely unaffected by the current whipping through the room. It was all she could do to keep from being sucked into the vortex, while he pressed on as if nothing had changed.

For him, it probably hadn't.

"I have a schedule for you," he said, walking to the desk and pulling out a folder. "You will read through these papers and be prepared to meet with the board first thing in the morning. We will discuss your duties then."

Rebecca stepped forward and clutched the folder, glad to have a new focus. Something hot and thick lurched to life in her sluggish veins. "That's it? No *Hi, how have you been?* No explanation?"

Ice-gray eyes regarded her dispassionately. "I owe you no explanation, Rebecca. I owe you nothing, in fact. Be grateful you're getting this much."

"I've been doing okay, thanks for asking, Alejandro," she said, ignoring him. "Or I was until yesterday. And you? How are you? Did you marry the woman you conveniently forgot to tell me about?"

"I did," he said coolly.

She blinked back tears. Ridiculous to still be hurt over such a thing, or to expect an explanation so many years after the fact. He was Alejandro Arroyo Rivera de Ramirez, international playboy, billionaire financier.

Women had always fallen over him. Always would.

And she'd been no different, had she? He hadn't been a billionaire back then, merely a famous man in his own country, making his way in a new business. *She'd* been the one with a privileged background, the one from hotel royalty. But she'd fallen hard for him; his betrayal still stung even now. She should have known better.

"You will be pleased to know we are divorced," he continued. "Alas, arranged marriages never work as planned."

"Good for her, for wising up."

"Like you did?"

A bitter laugh burst from her throat before she could stop it. "There was never a choice for me, Alejandro. You were already engaged."

"Promised, not engaged."

Rebecca scoffed, hoping he wouldn't see how the subject still affected her. "What is that? Spanish hair-splitting? The truth is you were to marry another woman when you so conveniently seduced me."

"You did not mind being seduced, as I recall."

Heat blossomed in her belly. Flooded her senses. Gathered between her thighs. "I was stupid—and blind to your true nature."

His square jaw flexed. He hitched a leg onto the corner of the desk, his custom-made trousers stretching tight against one hard thigh. "And just what is my true nature, *querida*?"

Danger saturated his voice, but she was too angry and hurt to heed the warning. No, what she itched to do was slap his sculpted profile. How dare he steal her company and then stand there and defend his actions of five years ago like he'd been the one wronged?

"You're a liar and a cheat."

She stood her ground as he stalked her. One arm snaked around her waist, yanked her against every last inch of his muscled body. The other hand gripped her jaw, forcing her to accept his kiss. Fire exploded in her veins when his lips pressed to hers.

Shock reverberated through her system. It was too much, too soon. She was still processing what it meant to see him again, to be flooded with conflicting emotions. She didn't want this, didn't need it.

Couldn't resist it for much longer.

Her hands went to his chest of their own volition, whether

to push away or touch him she wasn't sure. She marshaled what was left of her willpower and pressed her palms against a granite wall. He simply upped the ante, his tongue sliding along the seam of her lips, teasing her with remembered bliss.

She gave one last push. But he smelled good, felt good, and—

There would be time for recriminations later. Besides, nothing was ever as good as the memory. Surely one kiss would inoculate her to Alejandro's masculine charm. It was just what she needed to prove to herself he no longer meant a thing to her.

Her mouth parted and his tongue slipped inside. *Big mistake.*

But it was too late. She shuddered as she met him stroke for stroke. Was she out of her mind? She had to stop—but she didn't want to. Not yet. For a moment she was flooded with memories—his mouth on hers, his naked skin beneath her fingers, their bodies moving together in perfect rhythm. Ecstasy unlike any she'd ever known. Happiness and love and a feeling of rightness.

One of her hands threaded into his hair, luxuriated in its obsidian crispness. His fingers slid beneath her blouse, teased her nipple through the lace of her bra. It budded under his touch, sensitive and painful and neglected.

She held on to his shoulders, all sense of time and place leaching away as she lost herself in the hot need he called up. She very much feared that if he pressed her to the floor right now, ripped off her clothes and impaled her with his hard maleness, she'd wrap her legs around him and hold on for the ride. Just to feel that perfect rightness once more, even if it was only an illusion.

But, no, it *was* an illusion. She had to stop this. Now—

He broke the kiss first. "You're still sizzling, Rebecca," he said, his breath hot against her moist lips. "And you are still a slut."

Her hand connected with his cheek before he could block the blow. He moved away from her, laughing. She thanked God for the fury coursing through her right now, because without it shame would have eaten her alive. How had she managed to lose every last shred of dignity she possessed the instant he kissed her?

"Then I guess we know where we stand," she said, her breath razoring in and out. She would *not* hyperventilate. Not now. Stupid to let down her guard like that, to feel any softness at all toward this man. "And now I'd like to go to the hotel and get some rest—if you're finished trying to humiliate me."

"Your room is upstairs."

She gaped at him. "I'm staying here? In your villa? Is that wise?" she added, on what she hoped was a cool note.

"I cannot possibly refuse paying guests simply to house an employee. You will stay here."

An *employee*. The word grated like nothing else ever had. Worse, it stung that he could kiss her so hotly and then act as though it was nothing more than a joke. "Fine. But don't you ever touch me again."

His mouth twitched. "Are you sure about that? You were not so chilly a moment ago. Were you not remembering what it was like between us?"

She lifted her chin. No sense lying, because he'd see right through it. "You're a fine lover, Alejandro, but you aren't the only man who knows his way around a woman's body. Men like you are easy to find if a woman knows where to look."

"And where would that be?" His look was half amused, half curious.

"I believe they like to hang out at resorts and fleece rich women out of their money."

His brows drew together. "You are calling me a gigolo?"

"Keep it in mind if the hotel thing doesn't work out."

He threw back his head and laughed. Rebecca had to bite her lip to keep from grinning at the sound. She'd always loved his laugh. But the last thing she needed was to share a light moment with this man. He'd just stolen her company and ruined her career. The thought was enough to harden her resolve.

He reached for the phone on his desk, touched a button. "Señora Flores will show you to your room." She was almost to the door when his voice stopped her. "And do not worry, Rebecca. I have no intention of ever again accepting what you offer each time you look at me."

Rebecca's spine snapped ramrod-straight. "What's that? Sudden death? Because if you see anything else, you *are* a deluded man."

"Do not make me prove you wrong again."

She gave him her best glare, the one she'd perfected as a woman working hard to succeed in a man's business. "Try me when I'm no longer jet-lagged, Alejandro. I promise you the response will be much different."

Alejandro returned to the villa late, having spent several hours at his sleek downtown office. He tossed his jacket across a chair in the master suite, loosened his tie and tugged it from his collar. He started to pour a drink from the bar in his room, but changed his mind and pulled on a pair of swim trunks instead. Right now he needed the release heavy exercise could bring.

He hadn't expected Rebecca Layton to get under his skin ever again. It was purely physical now, and yet it annoyed him nonetheless. He'd spent one month with her five years ago. One incredibly hot month that he couldn't seem to forget, no matter how he tried. He'd enjoyed her company like none other. Enjoyed the way she'd looked at him, the way she'd smelled like wildflowers, and her funny way of saying things that meant something entirely different in American than they did in the British English he'd learned.

He'd cared for her; he'd planned to marry her in spite of what his father expected. No matter what he told her now, he hadn't been promised at all; it had been his brother who was to marry Caridad Mendoza, not him. Until Roberto had died of a drug overdose in a Middle Eastern hellhole.

Still, Alejandro had no intention of taking his brother's place in the arrangement. He'd spent years fighting in the ring, making himself into something. His future had been bright and he'd choose his own wife. Rebecca Layton, daughter of a successful American hotel magnate, had been exactly the type of woman he needed to marry.

Until she'd betrayed him. An ex-bullfighter and fledgling entrepreneur wasn't good enough for the pampered heiress, apparently. The dirt, sweat and blood of the ring would never wash completely away for someone like her. She'd accepted him as her lover, sworn she loved him, and then tried to steal his future from under his nose.

Her betrayal had cost him more than he could ever make her pay. Taking Layton International was only the beginning. He'd set it up carefully, made sure he would own her completely when it was done. It had taken years of planning and months of careful execution, but the culmination was here. Rebecca Layton would regret the day she'd crossed paths with him.

Alejandro pushed open the French doors and padded out to the pool. Lights flooded the water from below, illuminating the terracotta and turquoise tiles. He dove into the coolness, hoping it would drive the heat of kissing her from his memory.

Why had he succumbed to the urge? That one kiss had brought every bittersweet memory flooding back—especially when she'd clung to him, her soft moans coiling at the base of his spine, poisoning him with the urge to strip her naked and take her right there on the floor of his office.

"What in heaven's name do you think you're doing?"

Alejandro reached the wall, did a flip turn and propelled himself back toward the voice.

"Swimming." The water came up to his abdomen as he stood and looked at her.

"Not that," she said. "This." Rebecca thrust a handful of papers at him.

He ignored it and let his gaze wander over her sleek form. A red headband held her curls back from her face and matched the muted Hawaiian-print dress she wore. Slim legs tapered down to bare feet, but it was the circle of tiny white shells around one ankle that caught his attention. They caressed her ankle with every tap of her foot, kissed her bare skin like a lover.

Like he'd once done.

His gaze snapped to her face. "Those would be my plans to sell off a few of Layton's less lucrative holdings."

She took a step toward the pool. "The New York location? *New York?* Are you crazy?"

"Not at all. That hotel is small, outdated. It costs more in upkeep each year than it makes in profit."

The papers crinkled in her fist. "Why do you hate me so much?" she said, in a smaller voice than he would have expected.

She seemed almost bewildered. But it was a ploy. She would use anything to distract him, including sex. How well he knew that about her.

Her *poor little me* act angered him. "You know why. You used me to get information. You slept with me, then stole what you learned about the London deal to grab it for yourself. That move nearly destroyed Ramirez Enterprises."

Ramirez Enterprises had been little more than bravado and a dream back then. But losing the Cahill Group's financing had destroyed far more precious things than his fledgling enterprise. He wasn't about to tell her what she'd really cost him—what she'd forced him into to save everything.

She tilted her head to one side. "I didn't…"

"Didn't what?" he said, when she stopped speaking and stood there gazing off into space.

"You're lying." She crossed her arms and glared down at him. "You couldn't possibly be wiped out by one deal gone bad."

Of course she didn't realize how he'd struggled. She'd never struggled for anything a day in her life. From her first moments everything had been handed to her on a silver platter. He very much enjoyed being the one to take it all away.

Alejandro pressed his hands on the pool deck and levered himself out of the water. She took a step backward as he suddenly towered over her. He wanted to grab her, wanted to yank her into his arms and plunder her sweet mouth again. He turned away before his body betrayed his reaction to her. "Things were less certain then."

"So you bought a controlling interest in my company and now you plan to sell off my hotels one by one?"

Grabbing a towel from the lounge chair, he wiped his face dry before giving her a dangerous smile. "Only the unprofitable ones, *querida*."

"La Belle Amelie was the first hotel my father opened after he married," she said. "He named it for my mother."

Alejandro finished drying off and tossed the towel aside. She looked at him like he'd kicked her puppy. He hated it, hated the way she made him feel. But she was oh so good at manipulating him, wasn't she?

Never again.

"It goes."

Her laugh was bitter. "To think I once believed—" She shook her head, inched her chin higher. Met his gaze firmly. "I'll buy it from you. Give me a couple of weeks to put together the financing and I'll—"

"You once believed what?"

"Make you a good offer."

"Believed what, Rebecca?"

"Did you hear what I said? I want to buy La Belle Amelie. What I believed is of no consequence."

"Did you think I would marry you after a month together? Is that why you left?"

"God, no!"

She took another step back and he realized he'd been stalking her. He moved casually toward the edge of the pool, gave her space. The restless energy in him still demanded release, pounded through his body in waves. The hum was almost sexual, primal. Not much different from the way he'd felt whenever he'd faced a bull in the ring. He wanted to conquer, subdue, triumph.

"I left because you were engaged, Alejandro." Her chin fell as she studied the tiles at her feet. "I thought you were an honorable man. That's what I once believed."

If he'd been gored by a bull he'd have felt less pain. Less anger.

The unbelievable nerve of this woman.

"You dare to question my honor when it was you who left—*you* who went to London and talked the Cahill Group into backing you instead of me? I spent *months* putting that deal together and you yanked the rug from under me. No, I will never sell La Belle Amelie to you!"

Alejandro dragged in a breath, willed calm to replace the seething fury roiling inside him. "I'll have it demolished first, Rebecca. You can pick through the rubble and see what you can salvage then."

She remained unnaturally silent, her slender form shaking. He'd expected fury. Tears maybe. Pleading if she thought it would work. Sex as a last resort.

But the last thing he ever expected was for her to tackle him.

CHAPTER TWO

EVERYTHING went wrong the instant Rebecca lunged. Fury ate at her gut like battery acid. She'd planned to shove his arrogant carcass into the pool and go back to her room. And then she was going to call financier Roger Cahill. What Alejandro accused her of couldn't possibly be true.

Except the momentum required to throw Alejandro off balance tipped her too far forward. Her arms windmilled like crazy before she lost the fight and splashed down, landing on fifteen stone worth of angry Spanish male.

Something collided hard with the top of her head, and then she was sinking beneath the surface. She sucked in a breath, gulped chlorine. She needed to fight her way back up, needed to kick hard and breach the liquid barrier above her. But she couldn't seem to do it. Her limbs wouldn't cooperate.

How ironic to die in Alejandro's pool. The last thought rattling through her brain was that if there were any justice in the world, he'd get blamed for her death.

A second later, air burst into her lungs. She coughed sharply, spitting up water. Her head lolled against something hard and warm.

Alejandro.

"*Querida*, speak to me," he urged in a harsh voice.

Her back pressed down on a hard surface and she realized he'd laid her on the tile beside the pool. A moment later he hovered over her, his hands bracketing her head, water dripping from his skin onto hers.

She coughed again, her throat raw and burning. A sob welled up from somewhere inside, but she refused to give in to it. She gulped it back and stuffed it down deep. The last thing she would ever do was show weakness in front of this man.

"Rebecca, *amor*, say something. Call me a name if it pleases you."

"Arrogant idiot," she sputtered, though it came out as little more than a whisper. "Foolish Spaniard."

He grinned down at her. "I said one name, did I not?"

Her heart lurched. Not a good thing. "It makes me happy, calling you names."

It also made her happy to see him smile at her, but that was a piece of information she had no intention of sharing. One tear slipped from the corner of her eye and blazed a hot trail down her temple. She'd only been here a few hours and already a part of her longed for what used to be. *Get over it, Becca. He's not the right man for you, never was. He used you, same as Parker Gaines did.*

"What happened?" she asked, dashing the tear away with her fingers.

"I was trying to move out of the way when you fell on top of me. Your head connected with my elbow."

"Oh."

His fingers spanned her skull, probing softly. He was so close his breath whispered over her skin, sent a shiver skimming. "No bumps. I think you will live."

"Sell me the hotel, Alejandro," she urged, her eyes searching his. "It means nothing to you."

"And everything to you."

"Yes." She pulled a deep breath into her lungs, savoring

the sweet night air, forcing herself to go on though her throat was raw. "They built it together. He knew she missed Paris, and he gave it a French theme. There are family antiques in the hotel even now."

"You may have them." His eyes were flat, the concession seeming to cost him a great deal to say. "I won't prevent you from taking what is sentimental to you."

"The *hotel* is sentimental to me. I—" she swallowed "—I was born there. I beg you to reconsider."

His gaze slid down her body, over the wet dress clinging to every curve. One dark hand settled on her thigh, traced the outline of her leg, moving slowly up to her hip. His touch burned her, even through the layer of wet material between them. Mercy, what those fingers had done to her the last time they'd been together.

Rebecca bit her lip.

"To what lengths are you willing to go, *bella*, to secure your hotel?" His look was intense, as if a word or a nod from her would set in motion a seismic event that could not be stopped until they sprawled together in bed sated, replete— utterly ruined.

Her heart tapped hard inside her chest. His head descended in slow motion to her throat, his tongue pressing against an erratic pulse-point. "You want this," he murmured. His fingers spread over the wet material on her thigh. Her skin was cold from the pool and the night air, but his hand sizzled where it touched, branding her.

Once she would have welcomed his touch. Would have opened herself to him and reveled in the way he made her feel. Part of her still wanted to.

But she couldn't. It would cost her too much.

"No," she said softly. And again, stronger, "No."

His head lifted. His eyes searched hers, almost as if he couldn't believe what she'd said. Oddly, it gave her courage.

She pushed him away, satisfied when he rocked back, breaking all contact between them.

She lifted herself onto her elbows, and then to a sitting position when her head no longer spun. "I will buy it from you, Alejandro. I won't sleep with you for it."

"My, how you've changed." Sarcasm thickened his voice. "You weren't so principled five years ago."

"It's funny that you talk about principles when you were the one with a secret fiancée. Or was I the secret mistress?"

He unfolded from the tile deck, rose to his full height. "The only secrets were the ones you kept while you lied to me about your true reasons for being at the Villa de Musica."

Rebecca shook her head softly, stopped when a wave of nausea threatened. "You're unbelievable, Alejandro. You say I lied to you and stole your deal, but *you* were the one using me to learn how to expand your reach beyond Spain—"

"What?" He looked incredulous, his voice snapping into the night like a whip.

Rebecca shoved herself to her feet. The movement was too quick, and she almost sank to the ground, but Alejandro reached out and steadied her.

"I'm fine," she said, shrugging away from his touch. "We talked all the time, Alejandro. You asked me about every detail of the business, and I told you all I knew. You used *me*."

His hand dropped away. "I did not need *you* to succeed, Rebecca," he said coldly. "That I now own Layton International is proof of that, do you not think?"

She wrapped her arms around her wet body, her teeth beginning to chatter though she was burning up with fury on the inside. No, he hadn't needed her at all. Not in the way she'd wanted anyway. "You got lucky."

"Lucky? I make my own luck, *querida*. I don't wait for chance."

One temple throbbed with the beginnings of a headache.

He'd gotten lucky because her father had made mistakes, taken risks. If making his own luck meant watching Layton International like a panther and pouncing when they were crippled beneath the weight of obligations, then fine. He hadn't left anything to chance.

The exhaustion of the day sat like a lead weight on her shoulders. She just wanted to go to her room and pretend she was anywhere but here. With her ex-lover. Her ex-*love*.

"If you give me a few days, I'll put together a fair offer for La Belle Amelie."

He snapped his towel from the chaise, where he'd dropped it the first time. "You may have the family antiques, Rebecca, but the hotel is not negotiable."

"You just offered to let me buy it if I'd sleep with you."

He laughed. "No, I asked to what lengths you would go for the hotel. I did not say I would accept the offer."

Rebecca grabbed the papers she'd tossed onto one of the chaises. Then she spun to face him again, the documents crumpling in her chilled fist. "You can't deny you were aroused, Alejandro. If I'd said yes, we'd be in bed right now."

He looked bored. "I'm a man. A woman pressed against my body causes a reaction, *sí*. This is true of many men, I believe."

"Some more than others, apparently. I should have believed the stories I read about you. When you weren't fighting bulls you were bedding every woman in sight. I could have saved myself a lot of trouble."

The look he gave her was sharp. "The press enjoys telling tales. If I'd bedded half the women they accused me of, I'd have been too tired to fight and the bulls would have won."

"Well, it certainly didn't stop you from sleeping with me and a fiancée at the same time. Were there others too?" She flung the words at him, surprised at the vehemence knotting her throat. For years she'd thought of the face-to-face confrontation they'd never had. Would he have denied it if she'd given him the chance? Would he have apologized? He'd tried to convince her over the phone that he was not engaged. But his denials had fallen short because the truth was irrefutable.

"There was no one but you."

"You were engaged," she said, forcing the words past the wedge of pain in her throat. "I think that counts as someone else."

"I was *not* engaged."

"But you married her anyway. How convenient."

He took a step toward her, menace rolling from him in waves. "I married her because of you—because you stole from me and left me no choice."

This time she stood her ground. "I didn't steal anything, Alejandro. That's a lie."

"Of course you would say that. But it does not change the truth. When the Cahill Group informed me of their decision, they said they were investing in Layton International instead. Do you intend to tell me Roger Cahill lied?"

Rebecca tried to remember exactly what had happened then. She'd left Spain and gone to London to meet with Roger, at her father's direction, about a financing deal. They had not discussed Ramirez Enterprises. She would have remembered since the pain of Alejandro's betrayal had still been so raw.

"We were working with Roger on a South American deal. What he and his investors decided about you had nothing to do with us."

Alejandro snorted. "You expect me to believe that? Layton International wanted to shut out the competition. You tried to ruin me, or at least contain me to Spain."

"No," she said softly. "There was no reason. You weren't important enough."

He stiffened as if she'd dealt him a body-blow. "Or good enough, *sí*?"

"That's not what I meant." Ramirez Enterprises hadn't

been big enough to be a threat, but he didn't give her a chance to explain.

"I know what you meant, *querida*. How difficult it must have been for you to endure my touch. To sacrifice your body for the sake of your precious Layton International." He stalked closer until he towered over her—so close she could feel the heat of his skin, could smell the mixture of chlorine and male that threatened to overwhelm her senses. "You did a fine job of playing the whore, Rebecca. You were quite natural at it. But do not worry that you will ever need to lie beneath this dirty *torero* again. There are plenty of women who find it no chore to do so."

His words stung. "I slept with you because I wanted to. No other reason."

"Yes, tell yourself that if it makes you feel better."

Rebecca took a step away from him, her belly churning with hurt and anger. How dare he question her feelings, her integrity. He suggested she'd thought he was beneath her, unworthy of her because of what he'd been. God, it was untenable! "I *loved* you, Alejandro," she whispered fiercely. "You—"

"*Silencio!* I will not listen to your lies." He wrapped the towel around his waist and stood with fists on lean hips. Moonlight limned the hard contours of his chest, glistened on the water that still dripped from his head and left a trail of silver down his skin.

"Nothing you say will change the past, Rebecca, nor the fact I own Layton International. Spend your time worrying about your job, and cease trying to convince me you ever cared for me. We both know the truth."

Señora Flores coolly informed Rebecca that breakfast was usually served on the terrace in summer. There would be no coffee or pastries delivered to her room, no matter how sweetly she asked. But the last thing she thought she could do right now was sit across from Alejandro and share a meal. In fact, if she managed to avoid him altogether that would make her day nearly perfect. He'd accused her of so much ugliness. Of sleeping with him for information, of stealing from him and of lying about being in love with him.

Oddly, it was the last thing that bothered her most. She'd been so naive. She'd fallen fast and hard, and then she'd let the words fall from her lips often and easily. And, though he'd never repeated them, she'd believed he had cared for her. Believed what they had was special.

Until his fiancée sent a wedding coordinator to his hotel suite. *A wedding coordinator.* The woman had invitation samples, possible menus and fabric samples for his tuxedo. And he'd still denied he was engaged.

She was the one who'd been wronged, damn him! The one who'd had her heart broken and the pieces pulverized beneath his boot heels. Previous experience should have taught her he was only using her for the information she could give him, for her status as Jackson Layton's daughter, but she'd denied the truth and carried on blissfully with the affair. And he accused *her* of betraying *him*? Was the man insane?

She'd wanted to call Roger Cahill last night, see if she could find out what really happened, but it had been too late when she'd returned to her room. Today, however, she would make that call. There must have been a reason the Cahill Group had pulled their backing. A reason that had nothing to do with her or Layton International. Alejandro might never believe it, but at least she would know the truth.

Until then, how could she go out on that terrace and face him like nothing had ever happened between them? Eating with him was too intimate, too much like the past. And after last night her nerves were scraped raw.

She briefly considered refusing to join him, but she was too hungry—and she definitely needed the caffeine. Rebecca ran a comb through her honeyed curls one last time, before twisting them into a knot and securing it with a clip. Then she smoothed a stray wrinkle from her cream pantsuit and grabbed her briefcase, before shoving on a pair of matching sunglasses and heading for the terrace. She didn't want Alejandro to see the dark circles beneath her eyes. He'd only gloat at her distress, and she was in no mood for it.

She passed through a large great room, with soaring ceilings and pale stucco walls. Dark Spanish timbers spanned the ceiling at regular intervals. Cool cream furniture and inlaid Syrian wood tables clustered on silk Oriental carpets near a giant fireplace. Priceless art graced the walls—a Bellini madonna, a Picasso etching and a Velázquez oil among them. Even at his best, her father could only have afforded one or two of those paintings. Alejandro must be very rich indeed to have such a collection.

She went through large double doors propped open onto the terrace. Alejandro sat in profile to her. His white shirt hung open casually, the paleness of the fabric in contrast to his sun-warmed skin. A gray suit jacket was draped across a chair, the expensive fabric gleaming richly in the dappled sunlight falling through the arbor. He spoke a rapid stream of Castilian into the phone wedged to his ear. He didn't look up as she approached.

A uniformed man held out a chair. Rebecca gave him a smile as she sank onto it.

"Coffee, *señorita*?"

"Please."

He poured a steaming cup for her while she helped herself to a slice of toast, spread it with jam and took a bite. She could eat a side of beef, she was so hungry, but the typical Spanish breakfast was toast and jam, or *churros* with a pot of chocolate. After polishing off the first slice, she fixed another, biting into it as she let her gaze roam the courtyard.

"You wish for eggs and bacon?"

The sudden English startled her, whipped her concentration from the hot-pink bougainvillea vines overflowing the arbor. Alejandro's attention was on her now, the phone resting on the table beside his plate.

"This is fine."

"You do not want something more American?"

"Toast is American." She avoided meeting his eyes.

Alejandro shrugged. "It is not a problem. If you wish for something more, you have only to say so."

She continued to eat her toast. In light of all they'd said to each other last night, she didn't want to be thankful to him for anything. Knowing she owed him for dragging her out of the pool before she drowned was bad enough. Though if he hadn't made her so angry she wouldn't have been in the pool in the first place.

"You slept well?"

"Well enough," she said, spreading a third slice with jam. Praying he wouldn't guess she'd done anything but. That her heart was doing double time and her nerve-endings sizzled simply from being near him.

Before she knew what he was doing, he was standing beside her. He removed the clip holding her hair back and dropped it on the table as he tunneled his fingers into the loosened strands.

"Alejandro—"

"Shh." His touch was gentle, sure—and as startling as ever. He was so close his scent invaded her senses. No chlorine this time. Just expensive soap and man. Her eyes drifted closed as warmth spread through her.

"Ouch!" Her eyes snapped open again.

"It's a small bump," he said, his fingers exploring the swelling on her head. "Nothing serious."

Rebecca marshaled her resolve as awareness followed hard

on the heels of the warmth permeating her body. "Stop touching me," she said, batting at his hand.

"I have experience of these things, *bella*. You wouldn't want it to be serious, would you?"

"It's not. Leave me alone."

A second later, he whipped off her sunglasses. She tried to pull away, but he gripped her chin firmly, his eyes searching hers. "You did not sleep well."

Rebecca managed to jerk away. She snatched the shades from his hand and replaced them, praying he wouldn't see how she suddenly trembled with his nearness. How her skin sizzled and her blood hummed from the contact. "No thanks to you."

He returned to his chair and picked up his coffee cup. "It was you who pushed me into the pool, not the other way around."

"I wasn't talking about the pool. I'm talking about jet lag. I was in Hawaii yesterday, New York the day before. You could have given me more time to get here."

Hardly the full truth of why she hadn't been able to sleep, but that was all he was getting out of her.

He shrugged. "It's business. I do not have time to wait while you make your way leisurely around the world."

"No, I imagine stealing works best when done quickly."

His eyes glittered. "Careful, Rebecca."

"Or what? You'll drown me in your pool?" She knew she went too far, but she couldn't help it. Her bitterness from his accusations of last night boiled beneath the surface.

He set the cup down and stood, tossing his napkin onto the table. "We leave for the office in ten minutes. Be in the car if you wish to salvage anything of Layton International."

"Is that even possible? Or do you plan to sell it off piece by piece just to hurt me?"

He grabbed his jacket from the chair. "You will have to wait and find out. There is no other option, *sí*?"

Rebecca set the toast down, no longer hungry. "You really like being the one in control. You're enjoying this very much, aren't you?"

Alejandro's smile sent a chill skimming down her spine. "You have no idea, Señorita Layton."

Ramirez Enterprises was housed in a sleek glass-and-steel building in Madrid's financial district. The ride took over an hour in the thick traffic congesting the city's heart. The limo crawled like a beetle, inching forward until an opening appeared, then shooting between narrow gaps that had Rebecca cringing each time, expecting the scrape of steel on steel. By the time the car pulled into the drive in front of the building and a doorman appeared, Rebecca was exhausted.

When Alejandro exited the car, Rebecca on his heels, a cadre of men and women with cameras rushed forward. Flashes snapped, and Rebecca instinctively pasted on her public persona. Growing up with a wealthy father and a social butterfly mother had at least given her unfailing poise when the media appeared. It didn't happen to her much anymore, but of course Alejandro was a famous man in his own country. They'd been photographed often when she was last here. In fact, he'd gotten more attention than a pop star. She'd have thought it would have lessened now that he'd been away from bullfighting for so long, but apparently not.

"Señor Ramirez," the reporters called in unison. "Señor Ramirez."

Alejandro stopped, smiling broadly. He said a few words in Spanish, which caused several of the reporters to laugh.

"Can you tell us about the accusations of impropriety with construction permits in Dubai?" a man said in German-accented English.

"We are working with the Dubai authorities to get to the

bottom of the matter," Alejandro said smoothly. "I expect to begin construction very soon."

"You've been accused of bribing officials and short-circuiting the process. How do you answer that charge?"

His smile never wavered. "I deny it, of course. If you will excuse me, my business awaits. Miss Layton?" he said, turning to where she stood near the car.

"Rebecca Layton?" someone said. "Of Layton International?"

Alejandro faced the cameras again. "I have recently acquired Layton International, as you will have seen if you read the business section. Miss Layton is here to ensure the smooth transfer of her former company's holdings."

Former company. Rebecca's smile ached at the corners.

"How do you feel about the takeover, Miss Layton?"

Alejandro's smile didn't waver, but he shot her a warning glance. *To hell with him.*

Rebecca stepped forward. "I'm not happy about it, you may be assured. Layton International has been in the luxury hotel business for over a half century. We had hoped to continue, and were pursuing projects guaranteed to bring the Layton brand of luxury to new markets. This takeover is not the outcome we'd hoped for."

The reporters buzzed. One question rose above the others. "Do you suspect any impropriety in the acquisition process?"

Rebecca clasped her hands together in front of her. She knew it made her look innocent and somewhat vulnerable. "No—that's not possible, is it? The laws of our nations are very specific in regards to company stock and corporate mergers. Though Señor Ramirez might have wished to act immorally, I'm sure he did not do so."

The questions rose to a fever-pitch. Rebecca strained to hear a single one over the din, but Alejandro appeared at her side, his hand on her elbow.

"That's all for now," he said, ushering her toward the sleek glass doors of the building.

She resisted the urge to smile when the doors closed behind them, leaving them in the quiet of a polished lobby. A pretty receptionist greeted them warmly. Alejandro nodded his head to the young woman and propelled Rebecca toward an elevator. Her shoes clicked across black marble inlaid with shiny gold squares. She briefly wondered if they were real gold—if Alejandro would dare to display his wealth so garishly. A uniformed man greeted them as they passed inside a private elevator, then pressed a button and exited, leaving them alone as the gleaming doors slid closed.

"What the hell do you think you're doing?"

Rebecca leaned back against the brass rail and tried not to look like the cat that ate the canary. "What do you mean? I told them you did everything legally." Legally, but not morally. She had no doubt he'd understood what she'd said out there.

His gray eyes flashed. "You know very well you are jeopardizing our stock value with comments such as those."

"I'm sure you'll recover from the dip."

"Yes, but will I need to shed a few assets to keep earnings on projection?"

Her heart thumped at the threat, but she remained coolly unaffected on the outside. "*Did* you pay bribes in Dubai?"

"Do you think I would admit it to you if I had?"

She spoke before she could talk herself out of it. "You've grown fast over the years. I've wondered how you did it, but perhaps the secret to your success has little to do with business acumen and everything to do with your willingness to play dirty."

His gaze sharpened. "You'd like to think so, no doubt. But I assure you everything I've gained has been earned through hard work. Unlike yourself, no?"

His reaction was not as harsh as she'd expected, but it sliced deep. It was a charge that stung, but not one she could deny. At least not in any way he would understand. She'd had to work hard to prove herself to her father, to prove that a daughter would be every bit as good as a son when it came to captaining the family business. Harder than anyone would ever know.

She would not, however, share those struggles with Alejandro—or indeed with anyone. The memories of what she'd endured were too painful.

His look was telling. "How it must anger you to know your fate is in my hands. Perhaps you should be nicer to me? Encourage me to be gracious? How is it you say in America? That you must use honey to get the flies, not vinegar?"

She stiffened. "Don't you dare insult me by pretending I have a chance. You've already made up your mind, so why not just tell me what you want and be done with it? It's clear you have a plan, regardless of what I say or do. Save us both the hassle."

His gray gaze bored into hers. "What makes you think this is a—what was the word?—*hassle* for me?"

She speared her hair away from her face, having left the clip on the breakfast table. "I mean that since you already know what you want from me, let's just get right to it and skip this other stuff."

She sounded brave, though she was anything but. He could fire her here and now, put her on a plane and send her back to New York with nothing more than a bad case of jet lag and a rapidly dwindling bank account. She probably shouldn't have baited him with her statement to the reporters, but she was tired of being at his mercy. She wanted this nightmare over, wanted her company back and her life free of this man.

"Get right to it?" he said softly. "Skip the foreplay? Sometimes this is a good idea."

Rebecca's breath caught at the sensual undertone of his

voice. Was she imagining the heat in his gaze? The elevator seemed suddenly too small to contain the two of them.

"But not always," he said, his voice caressing the words. "You may plead your case in front of my board."

"They will vote as you want. What's the point?" she said, her voice far huskier than she would have liked.

"Maybe." He reached into his jacket and pulled out his PDA, frowning at the screen. The sexual tension emanating from him died as if he'd flipped a switch. He clicked the wheel, scrolling through the information there, shutting her out.

Rebecca gripped the railing, stunned both at the immediacy of her reaction and at his ability to turn off his own response. Because he *had* wanted her. She'd seen it. Hadn't she? Or was this simply another part of his game?

Unbidden, images of him flashed into her head. The jagged scar of a bull's horn slicing across his rib cage, the taut ripple and glide of muscle when he moved, the impressive jut of his erection. The ecstasy on his face when she straddled him and drove them both out of their minds with her slow thrusts.

He'd accused her of enduring his touch for the sake of her family business, of seeing him as nothing more than a bull-fighter dirty from the ring. If only he believed that she'd truly loved him, how sexy she'd found him in spite of the barbarity of his former profession.

Standing in this elevator in his custom-fit suit, he was as far from the glittering garb of a matador as any man could be—and yet she still saw the bullfighter beneath the polish. The raw, hungry, intense man who could stand in a ring with one ton of angry bull barreling toward him and never, not even once, flinch. This was a man who could stare death in the face and not blink.

After their affair had ended, she'd actually gone through a torturous phase of tracking down and watching his recorded fights. Holding her breath while the bull charged, while the cape swept down, then whirled away as Alejandro went up high on his toes and plunged his sword home. She'd thought it barbaric, and yet Alejandro had once explained, when she'd been tracing his scar in the aftermath of their lovemaking, how honorable the fight was for both man and bull. It wasn't her kind of thing—and yet there was a beauty in it.

A beauty in him.

She closed her eyes, remembered the heat of him, of the two of them twined together in his sheets. It had all gone so wrong, so horribly wrong. And she wasn't the same person she'd been back then—the same starry-eyed girl with dreams of love and a life with the most magnetic man she'd ever met. The world had certainly taught her the folly of those beliefs, hadn't it?

The elevator glided to a halt, the doors whispering open to let them into a spacious private office. Overstuffed chairs and a sleek sofa sat beneath a wall of books. A chrome and glass desk was positioned in front of floor-to-ceiling windows that ran the length of one wall. Alejandro went behind the desk and sat down without looking at her.

In the distance, the twin glass and steel structures of the Puerta de Europa leaned toward each other across the busy Paseo de Castellana. Much closer, the giant Estadio Santiago Bernabéu, where Madrilenians flocked to watch their soccer team, squatted against a bright blue sky.

"The board meeting will be in an hour. I suggest you prepare." He picked up the phone and spoke to someone. A second later, a pretty woman opened the door.

"Please escort Señorita Layton to a desk, Maria."

Rebecca followed the woman without another word, smiling and giving her thanks when Maria deposited her in a small, windowless office. Though she needed to prepare for the meeting, she first placed a call to the Cahill Group's offices in London. Roger was out of town until tomorrow, so she hung up and clicked open her briefcase. A glance at the clock told her she had fifty minutes left.

She didn't know what she'd encounter in that boardroom, but she wasn't going down without a fight.

When she was finally called to the meeting, more than an hour after she'd been told she would be, she was ready. She'd spent the last two hours completing her projections, dragging her finance people out of bed to give her numbers, and making sure her arguments were sound. Layton International would be out of the red in six months if she were allowed to continue on the path she'd chosen.

And though it burned her up to have to humble herself to these people, to explain her plans and defend her actions, she had no choice. She had to keep her company intact until she could somehow manage to get it back.

But the board meeting went exactly as she'd predicted. What Alejandro wanted, the board would do. If he decided to dissect her company limb from limb, he was within his rights to do so.

Rebecca shoved papers into her briefcase as the board filed out. She was on dangerous ground here. She was only technically still CEO until Alejandro decided otherwise.

A wave of apprehension rolled through her. And he *would* decide otherwise. She had no doubt. He was simply dragging this out to torture her.

How could she be the one who lost the company started by her grandfather? No matter that her father had taken out astronomical loans and pledged every last share of stock as collateral, she was still the one in control when the axe fell. She should have stopped it.

How? a little voice asked.

It didn't matter how. She should have simply *known* what to do. Her father would have.

Rebecca pinched the bridge of her nose, breathed deeply.

No—no one could have gotten them out of this mess. She simply had to deal with the situation as it was. She had to protect Layton International and the people who depended on her for their jobs.

"Why did you make me go through with that?" Rebecca demanded, frustration and anger churning together.

Alejandro shrugged a shoulder, his lazy stare infuriating. "If you do not like your new position, you can always quit."

Rebecca snapped her briefcase closed, then stood and stared down at him as coolly as she could muster, given the erratic beating of her heart. "I'm returning to New York to do my job."

"You forget who is in charge here, Señorita Layton." Alejandro leaned back in his chair, legs sprawled out in front of him as he toyed with a pen on the table. He looked nothing like a billionaire and everything like a mischievous Greek god who'd deigned to dabble with the mortals again. "You work at my pleasure and you leave when I say so."

"You don't own me." Her voice was little more than a whisper.

"Oh, but I do."

He meant it. She could see that. And he intended to make her suffer for it.

"What did I ever see in you?" she forced out past the knot in her throat.

For some reason that got his attention. He climbed slowly to his feet, his eyes glittering. The look on his face was pure danger. For reasons she preferred not to explore, a tiny thrill shot through her.

She straightened her spine, refused to back down as he moved closer. "What are you going to do? Kiss me again?" Her voice was huskier than she would have liked. The thought of him kissing her, pressing his body against her, wasn't nearly as repugnant as she wanted it to be.

Was she crazy? She didn't want to remember what it was

like between them, how much she'd once loved him. To feel anything at all for him, besides hate, was to betray everything her family had ever done for her.

"Would you like that, *querida*?" he said, moving toward her with lethal grace. "My mouth against yours?"

"No!" She resisted the urge to slink away. Where would she go? Against a wall? No, she'd stand here, take whatever he dished out. Give as good as she got. He might own her company—own *her*, in fact—but he would not control her. If he kissed her, she would remain cold and unresponsive.

She *would*.

"Your body says otherwise." He practically purred as his finger grazed her cheek. She was proud when she didn't betray herself with even the hint of a shiver. She stood stone-still and endured his touch. His fingers left fire in their wake as they ghosted over her skin.

"You are flushed, Rebecca." His fingers fell away, his hot gaze dropping to caress her body inch by inch. He no longer touched her, but she felt like his hands were everywhere at once.

His eyes caught and held hers. He took a step closer, still not touching her, but invading her space with his overwhelming physicality. "Your nipples bud for me. Feel how they want my touch. Should I kiss them?"

"You're mistaken," she said, forcing herself not to glance down, not to see the proof of his words.

A sensual grin creased his handsome features. "I am never mistaken about such things. Your heart pounds for me. I can see it. It is like a frightened rabbit."

"You're standing too close. I don't like it."

He stepped in again, until the hard length of his body hemmed her against the conference table. He placed his arms on either side of her, trapping her. "I think you do. I think, in fact, that you want me desperately."

"You're wrong, Alejandro," she said, lifting her head to

look him in the eye and deliver what she prayed was a stern look. "I hate you. I *don't* want you."

And yet her skin sizzled from his nearness. Her brain threatened to disengage completely. Her body trembled in spite of her resolve; an ache bloomed in the feminine core of her, spread outward on currents of liquid heat.

Alejandro's smile was too knowing, too masculine. "*Sí*, I feel your hatred. It is very strong. Very frightening for me."

His head dipped toward her. Her eyes drifted closed and he chuckled low in his throat, a sound of male triumph. Any second he would kiss her. Any second she would allow it. In spite of all she'd said. She was too weak, too lonely and needy—

No.

She found the strength to lift her palms, to push against his chest. At the same instant a buzzer sliced through the room. Alejandro stepped away, Spanish curses—or so she assumed—falling from his lips as he reached for the phone.

"*Sí?*" he barked.

Rebecca snatched up her briefcase and purse. She had to get away from here. She had to get home, back to New York, before Alejandro stripped her of far more than her company.

Her hand was on the door when his fingers closed over her shoulder. She gasped as he spun her around, pressed her against the door, his hard thigh wedged between her legs. He gripped her chin, pushed her head back until she was staring him in the eye.

"You will not leave me again, Rebecca. I call the shots— *comprende*?" His voice was low, intense. She had the feeling his words were more than a statement of fact.

They were a vow.

In spite of the heat between them, a chill slid over her. "I'm going to the airport, Alejandro. There's nothing for me here."

His eyes were colder than frost as he let her go and took a step back. "Walk out that door and I will destroy Layton

International. Your employees will be without jobs, your hotels sold or demolished, your assets carved up and absorbed into Ramirez Enterprises. I will make sure you never work in this industry again. No one will *ever* hire you, Rebecca. Walk out and it's over."

The depth of his fury stunned her. She wished she had the strength to do it, to walk out and not give a damn. But she couldn't let him take away the livelihood of the people who depended on her. At this moment she didn't care about herself—being anywhere but here, with him, would be less painful to her—but she couldn't desert them.

"What do you want from me?"

He glared at her without speaking for so long that she wondered if he'd heard her. Just when she started to repeat the question, he turned away.

"All in good time." He flicked a hand as if shooing away a bothersome fly. "You may go now."

CHAPTER THREE

WHAT did he want from her, she'd asked. Alejandro stared at the blinking skyline of Madrid at night. His problems in Dubai should take precedence—he had a hotel to build and permits to straighten out before he could do so—yet he couldn't seem to get the problem of Rebecca Layton out of his mind while he worked late.

He reached for the sherry he'd poured over twenty minutes ago, took a sip.

Damn her and her lies.

It was her fault he'd married Caridad. He would never have agreed to it had Rebecca not left him. Had she not *stolen* from him.

It wasn't just that she'd yanked the safety net out from under him. While it would have taken him far longer to take Ramirez Enterprises global without the Cahill Group's backing, he still could have done it without Caridad's family contributing to his coffers.

No, what Rebecca's betrayal had confirmed was the folly of allowing emotion to rule his head. He'd cared for her, had sometimes even envisioned the children they would have if he'd married her. He'd grown up with parents whose daily emotional drama should have inured him to any hint of sentiment, but Rebecca's smokescreen of naive charm had pulled him into her web.

What a bloody idiot.

And then he'd returned to his suite one afternoon and found a severe-looking woman waiting for him and no sign of Rebecca. The woman had fanned open a thick folder and nattered at him about planning a wedding.

It had taken him several more minutes to realize that Rebecca's suitcases were gone. The woman had simply shrugged. "*Sí*," she'd said. "There was a pretty young woman. She wished you a happy marriage to Señorita Mendoza."

That was when it dawned on him. His father, the old fool, had been urging him to marry Caridad since Roberto's death. Arranged marriages were no longer commonplace, but they did happen from time to time. His father had seen it as a measure of his own importance to find a bride for his eldest son. Roberto hadn't had the guts to object, which Juan Ramirez had known full well. He'd never have tried it with Alejandro. But then Roberto died. Señor Mendoza had loaned his father a lot of money, and Juan intended to deliver his famous son as payment if it was the last thing he did.

Alejandro had steadfastly refused. Apparently Juan had decided to step up the campaign. The timing could not have been worse.

Alejandro's first thought had been to go after Rebecca. But she'd had a head start and he'd had no idea where she'd gone. His calls to her mobile phone had gone unanswered. Two days later she'd finally picked up. From London. She'd been cool and aloof, and he'd lost his temper. How dared she expect an explanation? All she'd needed was to accept that what he told her was the truth: he was not engaged.

Not surprisingly, she hadn't believed him. He'd realized later that his alleged engagement was merely a convenient excuse for her to do what she'd always intended to do. The next day Roger Cahill had told him they were backing Layton International instead.

Rebecca had said she loved him, but she'd lied. He wasn't good enough for her and never would be in her eyes.

You weren't important enough.

It had pricked his pride, sliced a wound in his soul, the knowledge that this woman he'd cared about had used him. He'd vowed never again to believe protestations of love from any female. So he'd agreed to marry Caridad. Why not? Her breeding and social standing were impeccable. She would be the perfect hostess, the perfect tycoon's wife, the perfect mother to his children.

He'd certainly been mistaken on that point. He could not have chosen a colder, more unfeeling woman for his wife if he'd tried.

Alejandro swallowed a mouthful of alcohol, welcomed the burn as it slid down his throat. Who could have guessed how much pain he would have to endure before his marriage was over? He'd never known such despair, such aching emptiness. Everything that had happened to him, everything that had sliced his soul to shreds and left him hollow inside, could be traced to that moment when Rebecca Layton had left him. If not for her, it would have turned out so differently.

He'd vowed long ago that every ounce of pain she'd ever dealt him would be returned to her before he was through. That was what he wanted from her.

Rebecca had no real destination as she wandered through Alejandro's darkened house. It was after ten, and everything was quiet. A small lamp burned on the desk in the home office she'd first seen him in yesterday. She went inside, thinking to find a book to read since she wasn't sleeping so well.

She studied the titles lining the bookshelves with interest.

What did Alejandro like to read? It surprised her to realize she hadn't known before. Hadn't known much about him, in fact, if she thought about it. He'd come far indeed in the five years since she'd last seen him.

But his fury and hatred stunned her. Clearly he believed she had ruined his deal with the Cahill Group. But even if it were true, which it was not, why would that be enough to make him hate her so much? The business world was often unfair. *Life* was unfair. Sometimes it was downright cruel. Plenty of times in the last few months she'd wanted to bury her head in her hands and scream at the unfairness that had left her in charge of Layton International so soon. The monstrous bad luck that had her father climbing on a tiny plane in Thailand so he could tour the resorts he'd just acquired.

But she hadn't. She'd picked herself up and dusted herself off and got back to work. There had been no other choice.

Most of the books were in Spanish. *Don Quixote*, naturally. *The Count of Monte Cristo* in English. Interesting. She started to reach for Dumas's tale of wrongful imprisonment and revenge, but another book caught her eye. This one had the word "Photos" emblazoned on the spine.

What sort of photos would a man like Alejandro find important enough to paste into an album? Bullfighting ones, no doubt. Curious, she pulled the book from the shelf and placed it on the desk in front of her.

She opened the cover and sank into Alejandro's chair, her knees no longer strong enough to hold her upright. A little girl smiled back at her. A beautiful black-haired child, with gray eyes and a smile so familiar it hurt to see it.

But to see it in a toddler?

His child. Without a doubt this girl was Alejandro's child. She had his smile, his eyes, the stubborn tilt of his chin. When he appeared in a picture with her, the resemblance was unmistakable. Tears sprang to Rebecca's eyes. Why? She wiped at them furiously, flipping pages until she came to a photo that made her heart stop. Alejandro holding the little girl on a beach. He was healthy and tanned, his smile glowing as he gazed at his daughter. The girl stared at whoever took the photo, a finger in her mouth, her eyes wide.

Rebecca chewed absently on a knuckle. He'd had a child after she'd gone back to America. He'd married the woman and had a beautiful little girl with her. Jealousy speared Rebecca like a poisoned barb. *You have no right*, she told herself. *You left.*

But she'd had to go. He'd been engaged.

He said he wasn't, a voice whispered. *You gave him no chance to prove it to you.*

She shook her head. If he hadn't been engaged, why had he gone through with it? You didn't marry someone and have a child with her if you weren't committed somehow.

Rebecca forced herself to flip more pages. It was mostly the little girl, though her mother appeared in a couple. Never smiling, that woman. Never looking anything other than irritated.

A nanny, perhaps?

But, no, the little girl had her mother's bone structure. Rebecca turned the pages faster. She could almost be glad that Alejandro had had a sour-faced wife if not for the little girl who was probably tugged between divorced parents even now. No child deserved to have parents who disliked each other.

At least her own parents had been in love, even if her father had never been home long enough to pay any attention to a disappointing girl-child who'd craved his affection and approval. Her mother, who'd been addicted to shopping and socializing, had often left Rebecca in the care of a nanny. She'd been a lonely, lonely child.

Who'd grown into a lonely adult. She swiped a hand beneath her nose, sniffed back her tears. *Get over it.*

On the last page of the album was an official-looking document, but it was in Spanish and she couldn't read it. *Certificado de defunción.* What did that mean?

"What are you doing in here?"

Rebecca's head whipped up at the angry demand. She'd been so focused she hadn't heard him come in. She slapped the album closed a little too hard—a guilty reaction at being caught going through his personal things.

Alejandro strode into the room and snatched the album from the desk. "You are never to touch this again, *comprende?*" He spun from her and disappeared through the door.

She sat in stunned silence. Whatever she'd expected, that hadn't been it. Why was he so upset with her? It didn't matter; she had to get out and get back to her room before he returned—before he confronted her with whatever nastiness was on his mind.

But she waited too long to move. Before she reached the door, Alejandro was back, looming in the entry, anger rolling off him in waves.

"You dare to go through my things? After what you did the last time?"

"I'm sorry," she said. Because she had, in fact, violated his privacy. She hadn't meant to, but when she'd seen the album she'd simply been too curious to stop. "Your daughter is very pretty, Alejandro. I'm sorry if I upset you by looking at her photos."

He passed a hand over his face, swore under his breath while shaking his head. It made no sense to her, but when his hand dropped away what she saw on his face twisted her heart. Pain like nothing she'd ever experienced. Longing and regret.

Loneliness.

He pulled in a ragged breath. "*Sí,* Anya was very pretty. She was the best thing I have ever done."

Was? Rebecca's heart squeezed, hard. Oh, dear God. The official document at the end was a death certificate. *Defunción*—death. How had she blundered so badly?

She swallowed the knot clogging her throat. "I'm sorry," she said again.

"Get out of my sight." The words fell like empty bullets onto the floor. Hollow, dull. He sounded suddenly very tired, very worn. Very unlike the vibrant man she knew.

She came out from behind the desk and walked to the door. He flinched when she put her hand on his arm. The movement saddened her. Once he would have welcomed her touch. No longer. "I'm sorry for your loss, Alejandro."

She truly, truly was. No one should have to endure such a thing. The experience had changed him. She could see that. It had made him harder, colder, less sympathetic than he'd once been. It explained so much and made her ache for him.

His hand closed over hers before she could pull it away, held it there as his pain-filled eyes raked her.

"You think I am like the lion with the thorn in his paw, yes? You think if you pull it out I will be forever in your debt?" As much as he tried, the malice was missing.

"I didn't say that."

"You didn't have to."

She swallowed. "No one should lose a child. I can't know your pain, but I'm sorry for it." She knew what it was like to lose a parent unexpectedly, but her father had at least had a life first. Alejandro's little girl never got the chance.

His fingers tightened. "You would offer to comfort me, perhaps? Take me to bed and make me forget?"

Rebecca couldn't speak. She watched him, her breath tight in her chest, her eyes filling with unshed tears. A part of her was ready to hold him, to let him take whatever he wanted from her. Another part—the angry, betrayed part—wanted to hold on to her fury at him. She was paralyzed by opposite urges.

Alejandro was not. "You can keep your pity and comfort to yourself, Rebecca Layton. I do not need it."

He let go of her hand.

"I'm sorry," she said again. Because there was nothing else to say.

"Go."

For once, she obeyed without question.

By the time Rebecca stood at the pool's edge and considered taking off her robe and underwear and going for a swim, it was nearly three in the morning. She'd tried to sleep. She'd turned on the television and watched a Spanish movie—not that she'd understood a word—and hoped it would bore her enough.

It hadn't. But was it jet lag or Alejandro that kept her awake?

She swirled a toe in the water and thought of the look on his face when he'd told her his child was gone forever. A hand drifted over her abdomen almost without conscious thought. Once she'd thought *she* would be the mother of Alejandro's children.

Her heart swelled with sorrow. His poor, poor wife. Rebecca had never spared any good will for the woman who'd crushed her dreams with her mere existence, but she hurt for the former Señora Ramirez now. Had their child's death torn their marriage apart?

Alejandro had been so angry earlier, so defeated. Not at all the man she knew. She'd had no idea what to say to him, no words to breach the barrier of anger and mistrust between them. She'd been so focused on her own problems since arriving; the shock of realizing he was very much as human and vulnerable as anyone else was hard to reconcile with the brutal tycoon who wanted to destroy her life.

His loneliness had reached out to her and she'd been almost powerless to resist it. In spite of the hurt, in spite of all he'd done to humiliate and control her, she'd felt in that instant like they shared a connection. A very, *very* dangerous feeling.

Rebecca blew out a breath. The night air was warm, the pool inviting. She hadn't come out here with the intention of swimming—if she had, she'd have worn her swimsuit—but the temptation to do so was strong. Or maybe she'd just slip her clothes off and sit on the terraced stone steps beneath the waterline.

What had happened to little Anya? She'd been such a beautiful child, so sweet-looking. Then again, weren't all babies sweet-looking? She didn't know much about babies, really. Tears threatened, lodging in her throat, a ball of pain she couldn't swallow. *Damn it, she had to stop thinking about this, about him.*

Rebecca slipped her robe off and tossed it onto a chaise. A second later her camisole and panties followed, and she hurried down the steps before she could change her mind. Goose bumps rose on her skin the lower she sank into the water. Though the air was warm, the pool was slightly cooler than she'd expected after dipping her toe in. She almost turned around and went back, but she forged on until she could sink onto the lowest step, the water right below her naked breasts.

Water lapped at her nipples and she sucked in her breath as they budded tight. It had been so long since anyone had touched them. She was tormented with sadness and hurt, yet she threaded one hand up her torso, her heart thudding, and softly pinched one of the peaks between her thumb and forefinger. Was it wrong to want to feel good again, even if only for a moment?

A sound from the direction of the arbor lodged her heart into her throat. She craned her head to try and see, her heart shooting into overdrive. Did Madrid have wild animals inside the city limits? Did burglars dare to rob someone as wealthy and powerful as Alejandro?

Maybe she should run into the house—but her feet refused

to move. What if it was nothing? She strained to hear any odd noises against the backdrop of ordinary night sounds, but the blood was so loud in her ears she couldn't separate any one sound from the others.

Until something scraped.

"Who's there?" she said, and immediately felt ridiculous. An animal wouldn't answer, and neither would an intruder.

She stared hard at the arbor, her heart skipping a beat as a shape unfolded itself from the darkness, growing bigger as the light caressed its shadow. A lifetime later, it resolved into the shape of a man.

A tall man, with dark hair and the body of a god, dressed in jeans and a dark T-shirt. Her heart went out to him.

"You are enjoying yourself, *no*?"

Rebecca pulled her knees to her chin to hide her nakedness, her skin flushing. "You scared me half to death, Alejandro. How long have you been there?"

"Long enough."

She nibbled her lip between her teeth, wanting to ask him if he was all right and yet sensing he would not welcome the question. "You could have announced yourself," she said instead.

And saved her the embarrassment sizzling through her now. It didn't matter that he'd seen her naked in the past, that he'd probably kissed every inch of her skin and shown her things no man ever had. To think he'd watched her the whole time—even when she'd let her hand trail up her body…

"I'd like you to go," she said, with as much dignity as she could muster. *Please, please go.*

His smirk told her he would do nothing of the sort. He settled into a chair, crossing one leg casually. An arm draped over the side, fingers rubbing back and forth against the chair's edge. "Why would I want to leave, Señorita Layton? It is my house, is it not? And I was here first."

"Then I'll leave. Would you hand me my robe, please?"

"No."

Frustration hummed beneath the surface. "Alejandro, please. What is the point in this?"

His eyes narrowed. "Are you uncomfortable?"

"I think you know the answer."

"Then perhaps that is the point."

Rebecca swallowed. "I'm sorry I looked at the photos. I didn't know it would upset you."

He made a rough noise. "You may apologize, but this does not explain why you thought it acceptable to go through my things in the first place. Looking for information you could use against me, Rebecca? Something you could sell to the press, perhaps? I assure you that you will not find anything."

"What? No!" She hugged herself tighter. It was disconcerting to argue with him while she sat here without a stitch of clothing. He lounged in the chair so casually, like there weren't oceans of pain between them. She had a sudden urge to be completely truthful with him, to try and bridge the gap somehow. "I want a chance to redeem Layton International, yes. If you would let me repurchase the stock, I'd be grateful. I'm not trying to hurt your business. I only want my company back."

He didn't say anything for a long moment. "How grateful?"

She couldn't tell by his tone how he meant the question. Was he baiting her? Making fun of her? Heat prickled her nerve endings. "Um, well, I think we could work out some profit-sharing. Perhaps even a partnership or two?"

He didn't answer. Instead, he got to his feet, tugged at the waist of his T-shirt with one hand. A moment later it fell to the tile deck. Rebecca's pulse skipped. "What are you doing?"

"Considering your proposal." He unsnapped his jeans, shrugged them down his lean hips in a graceful movement that had her blood pounding in her ears. When he stood at the edge of the pool in nothing but his briefs, Rebecca had to remind herself to breathe. She'd dreamt of that body for five years. Dear heaven, she remembered at the most inopportune moments what his flesh felt like pressed to hers, moving inside her. She'd even called her ex-boyfriend Alejandro once during sex. No wonder she'd been alone for the past year and a half.

Her mouth went dry at the sight of all that hard muscle and tan skin. "Wh-what proposal? What are you talking about?" And why did her head feel as if it were stuffed with cotton wool?

"How grateful would you be, *querida*?"

She cast her mind back over the conversation, tried to piece together what exactly he meant. And then her brain shut down and her jaw slipped open as the last of Alejandro's clothing fell away.

A second later he was in the water.

CHAPTER FOUR

ALEJANDRO swam toward her, idly wondering if she would shoot up the steps and into the house. If she did, then perhaps she wasn't as calculating as he thought. Perhaps she really hadn't known he was beneath the arbor, watching her.

He half hoped she would run. It would be nice to think she wasn't trying to use him this once, especially when his memories were so raw. After she'd left him in his office he'd gone for a walk in the grounds. Then he'd sat under the arbor and hoped his mind would quiet. It hadn't.

When she'd appeared, stealing through the night like a wraith, he'd watched her curiously. And then she'd dropped her clothes, like the calculating slut she was.

And, like it or not, her striptease had made him harder than the stone this pool was built out of. Which had no doubt been her intention. She'd played at asking him to leave, but he hadn't bought her act. The truth had emerged, of course, when she'd said she'd be grateful if he would sell her Layton International.

She didn't move as he stopped in front of her. He was both disappointed and pleased. He hadn't intended to touch her ever again, but that had been before he'd watched her strip down and caress herself.

Madre de Dios, he wanted to bury himself inside her right

this moment. Would she be as hot and tight as he remembered?

But, no, he would not give in to his body's demands. He would, however, prove to them both that she was a mercenary bitch who would do anything to get what she wanted.

"What are you doing?" she asked, still clasping her knees, her eyes wide. He didn't miss how her gaze dropped, shot back to his face. *Little Miss Innocent.*

The water caressed his hip bones, the evidence of her effect on him hidden beneath the surface of the pool. If she stood, however, she would see he was more than ready for her.

"I am giving you a chance to show your gratitude."

"You haven't given me anything to be grateful for," she shot back, her facade cracking.

"What would you like, Rebecca? La Belle Amelie?"

Her head dipped as she turned her gaze from him. Calculating, no doubt. "I won't sleep with you for a hotel."

"What if that is my price?" He knew she would break. She was simply trying to get more out of him first.

Blue eyes gleamed as she met his cool stare. "You're saying you will *give* me my hotel if I let you make love to me?"

Alejandro chuckled. So predictable. "What I wish to do to you right now has nothing to do with love."

She blinked. "How do I know you mean it, Alejandro? How do I know this isn't part of your game?"

"So you will accept if I am serious?"

She looked away again. "I didn't say that."

He reached for her hand. The contact of skin on skin sizzled into his brain, made his manhood leap in anticipation. She did not resist when he twined his fingers with hers and pulled her toward him.

Of course she didn't.

He took her into deeper water without looking back at her.

When he stopped and turned, the crests of her nipples were just below the surface.

She chewed her bottom lip, watched him warily.

"I will give you your hotel, Rebecca. You need only give me your body. Surely this is a fair trade?"

A moment later, her chin tilted up. Ah, so the imperious heiress had arrived.

"I want it all. I want a chance to buy back my stock."

Anger simmered deep inside though he smiled to cover it. He'd known she was playing him, hadn't he?

"I will consider it."

She took a deep breath. He had her now. She would not pass up the opportunity. If he'd told her yes, she would know he was lying. But if he offered to consider it, she would believe he could still be persuaded. And she would turn all her considerable charms toward convincing him.

He waited almost eagerly for her next move.

"I'm leaving," she said, turning away from him and stroking toward the closest ladder.

Not at all what he'd expected, but that only made the game more fun.

Rebecca swam for the ladder. What was she thinking, telling him she wanted everything if she gave in to his demands? She had absolutely no intention of making love to him for a hotel, or company stock, or anything else. She would not be brought down to his level. He believed her to be mercenary. Though a rebellious part of her wanted very much to be in his arms again, she would not give in to the temptation. Every nasty thing he'd ever thought about her would be justified in his mind if she did.

She reached for the ladder, put her foot on the first rung. Strong arms twined around her torso and pulled her against his body.

Oh, dear heaven, his *aroused* body.

The hard length of him was hot against her backside. In fact, every last inch of his skin seared her as he held her close. His fingers snaked across her belly; his other hand slid up to cup her breast, tested the weight of it in his palm.

She shivered with longing.

"I will give you the hotel, Rebecca. I will consider the rest, though perhaps we will need a repeat performance or two to persuade me."

His breath was hot in her ear, teasing her, tempting her with remembered bliss. It wasn't fair to want this man so much in spite of all he'd done, to turn to mush the instant he touched her.

She knew he only wanted her because she was here, because she was female, and because he knew she was vulnerable to him. She'd proven that when she'd let him lead her into the pool. If she'd truly wanted to get away she would have gone into the house the instant he entered the water.

She was an idiot, a lonely needy girl who still wanted to be loved by *someone* in her life. Was it asking too much to want what so many other people had?

What Alejandro had had with his wife and baby girl?

But, no, it was an illusion. Everything with him was an illusion, and she wouldn't allow herself to believe it ever again.

But he's hurting. He lost a precious child and he's so very different because of it. He needs you.

She gritted her teeth against the onslaught. *No.*

"I can't do it," she said, as much to convince herself as him. "I don't want to."

It was a lie, though she prayed he would not figure out the truth.

Alejandro turned her in his arms, pressed her against the side of the pool. The water was over her head here, so she had no choice but to cling to him. His dark head dipped down, his lips ghosting over her cheek, touching the shell of her ear.

"You want me, *querida*. You cannot deny this."

"I don't," she said desperately.

"Not even for your precious hotel?"

She started to shake her head, realized her mistake when her mouth grazed his jaw and he turned his head, his lips capturing hers. She moaned—but was it protest or acquiescence?—as her head fell back and her mouth opened beneath his. Whatever the reason, he took advantage of the lapse to tangle his tongue with hers. Wild, hot, sucking—their mouths devoured each other. Flame licked up her belly, blossomed between her thighs.

How could she possibly want this man after all he'd done? His loneliness called out to her, connected with her own inner feelings of isolation, tempted her in spite of her best intentions.

His hands slid down her buttocks, over her thighs, lifted them until she wrapped her legs around his waist, the hard length of him pressing against her center. Her body remembered all too well how wonderful it had been between them. He'd left his impression on every nerve, every cell. Five years had not been enough to erase it.

Even as she shuddered, part of her brain remained lucid, sent the message to drop her legs, to end this before it went too far. He lifted them again, urging her to open to him. He gave her no chance to refuse as his thumb glided between her thighs, found the hot, wet center of her.

Rebecca gasped. It had been so long…

Alejandro pulled back, gazed down at her with an expression that contained both surprise and confusion, as if he too were a little rattled by how quickly the situation was spiraling out of control.

"You are so hot for me. Like a flash fire."

Something inside her was breaking—breaking all her control and shattering her best intentions. She had to find her balance, had to resist the siren pull of him on her soul and her body before it was too late.

Panic set in, demanded she slow this thing between them before she was completely lost, before she gave in and did exactly what she knew she shouldn't do. Before she lost herself.

She blurted the first thing that came to mind. "La Belle Amelie."

Alejandro's expression froze. A second later, his smile turned cold. "Yes, of course. Ask me about your hotel."

He didn't stop touching her, didn't give her a chance to react before he slipped a finger inside her, stroked her hot flesh. Sensation spun her higher, rocketed her toward the peak.

But Alejandro's heart was no longer in it. She could see the disconnect in his expression. Icy anger had been replaced by cool neutrality. He was completely unaffected while she was close to meltdown.

Why had she mentioned the hotel? Stupid, stupid, stupid.

"Stop," she said, fighting her body's reaction, fighting him.

"Are you certain?" His thumb moved faster against her sensitive flesh, sent pleasure spiking.

"Yes, stop," she gasped.

Too late. A wave of sensation crashed over her long-neglected senses, hurtling her into forgotten pleasure. Her body left her brain behind as she quivered and moaned in his arms.

Alejandro didn't stop touching her, kept the pleasure spiking and cresting. His mouth touched hers. Softly, sweetly, completely at odds with the look he'd given her when she mentioned the hotel.

What was she thinking to have said such a thing?

"Alejandro," she gasped when he nuzzled her ear, whispering something in Spanish. She had to explain, had to make him understand. "About the hotel—"

She felt him stiffen.

"*Sí*, the hotel," he said, pushing away from her suddenly. Water dripped from his tanned skin, glistened over the molded perfection of his lips. Every line of his face was set in a hard angle as he glared at her. "Would you care to ask me for something else before you allow me into your body? Name your price, Rebecca, for surely I am desperate for you now and will give you anything you wish."

Ice dripped from his words, freezing the languid warmth swimming in her veins.

"That's not what I meant—"

"No, of course not. You meant to ask for more. How often have you lain on your back to get what you want from a man, I wonder?"

Rebecca shoved at his chest, forcing him to let her go. She gripped the ladder to keep from sliding beneath the surface. Her body still tingled from his touch, and yet she'd never felt more cold and alone in her life.

"How can you be so cruel?" she asked. "I'm not a cheap whore—"

"No, you are actually quite expensive—"

"Stop interrupting me!" she shouted, uncaring who might hear or come running to see what was going on. "You push and push, Alejandro, and you have *no* idea what you're talking about." She sucked in a breath to stop her angry tears before rushing on. "You're a cruel, bitter man that no woman could *ever* love for very long! It's no wonder your wife left you after Anya died—" Rebecca slapped a hand over her mouth.

A muscle ticked in his jaw as he glared at her. And yet something in his hard stare had changed. There had been a moment, when she'd said it, that she would have sworn he flinched. That defeated look crossed his features again, but only for a second.

"Oh, God, I'm sorry. I didn't mean to say that."

"*Sí*, you said exactly what you wanted to say." He crowded

her against the ladder so suddenly she gasped. "And now I say to you that you are a whore who will sleep with anyone, tell any lies, in order to win. You and I are much alike in our willingness to do whatever it takes, *no*?"

Her chest rose and fell, her emotions on the edge of a precipice. "I am *nothing* like you."

"You only lie to yourself, Rebecca, because I know the truth." He leaned down until his breath was hot on her cheek. "Remember when you think to fool me again that I am twice as ruthless as you. I will *always* win."

Sadness gripped her as she looked at his proud, cold, hard features. He'd changed so much in five years. The life and spark of him was extinguished, leaving nothing but a shell. "How can you call it winning, Alejandro, if it makes you so miserable?"

Alejandro sat in the plush leather club chair and buckled his seat belt as the pilot announced they were next in line for take-off. Moments later the Ramirez jet lifted off, banking to the right to give him a spectacular view of the financial district and, far beyond, the residential section where his villa lay. Where Rebecca still slept.

Was it only three hours ago he'd held her in his arms and watched the ecstasy on her face when she'd shattered? *Dios*, in that moment he'd strongly considered forsaking his vow not to bed her. She was so vibrant, so alive and warm—she pulsed with life in his arms.

And he'd wanted to feel it with her. After his divorce, he'd tried to lose himself in a string of women, to forget what he'd lost when he'd lost his child. Every encounter had been empty, cold. He'd thought he would feel relief when it was over, but he'd felt nothing. *Nothing*.

His heart was frozen. He'd felt nothing since Anya died. Until Rebecca had walked into his house and glared at him with all the hurt and loneliness she'd ever felt shining in her eyes.

He wanted to ruin her. And he wanted to possess her. It made no sense, though he usually prided himself on making decisions based on sound judgment.

It was simply a physical need. He'd almost forgotten she had an ulterior motive until she made the mistake of mentioning the hotel. Another moment, another hot kiss, and he'd have been so deep inside her he'd still be entangled in bed with her now, instead of flying to Dubai to meet with the government officials holding up his construction.

The bell dinged to signal the jet had reached ten thousand feet, but he made no move to turn his phone back on or to power up his laptop. She'd asked why he was miserable. It had shocked him. He'd wanted to deny it, but he hadn't. He'd wanted to tell her she was terminated, to go back to New York and her life there. But the words hadn't come. And she hadn't moved, had merely clung to the ladder and stared at him with a pitying expression on her face.

Madre de Dios. He hadn't felt so exposed since Anya's doctors had stared at him with that same pitying expression.

He would not allow Rebecca to get inside his head. It shouldn't even be a possibility! No, what he had to do was becoming clear. He had to take her into his bed, had to dominate her as completely personally as he had professionally.

It was simply another layer to his revenge. He would bed her, let her think she had him exactly where she wanted him, that she could manipulate him into giving her back her company, and then he would destroy her utterly.

Alejandro accepted a mineral water from a flight attendant as he opened his laptop. Decision made, he already felt a world better. Rebecca Layton would never defeat him. Never again.

Rebecca was quite relieved she didn't have to face Alejandro over a breakfast table, though she was somewhat surprised to learn he'd flown to Dubai. But now—oh, thankfully—*now* she didn't have to look at him and know he'd touched her so intimately, made her want to do things with him that in her right mind she'd never do again. She knew she couldn't allow her sympathy for his loss, for the pain and anger she saw in his eyes, to divert her from her goals. She *had* to keep Layton International safe and whole, and she had to find a way to get it back. It was all that mattered.

He'd left her no instructions while he was gone, had not revealed a single element to his plan for her company. So until the man fired her, or she convinced him to let her buy back her stock, she had a business to run.

Rebecca frowned at her reflection. After last night she had no illusions Alejandro would ever allow her to buy back her stock. The only way to retrieve Layton International would be if Alejandro suddenly found himself in trouble and needed to sell some assets. And, according to all her contacts, that wasn't happening. Ramirez Enterprises was a juggernaut. Not only that, but Alejandro would sell her company piece by piece if forced. He would never allow it to be bought whole, and certainly not by her.

Yet she couldn't simply give up and cower like a whipped puppy.

After a quick shower and something to eat, she phoned Roger Cahill again. She still needed to know what had happened five years ago, if there was even the smallest chance she could prove to Alejandro that she hadn't stolen his deal.

"Becca," Roger said when his secretary put her through. "I was just thinking about you. It's been a long time."

"Yes. Thank you for the flowers you sent to Dad's funeral."

He cleared his throat. "Jackson was a good man. I'm sorry I won't get to play a round of golf with him at St. Andrews this year."

"I know he would have enjoyed it."

"You mustn't blame yourself for losing Layton International," he said, launching straight into the heart of the matter. "When Jackson came to me, I told him it was a bad idea to stake so much on those Thailand resorts."

Rebecca's mouth twisted. If only the bank that had loaned him the money had felt the same. The bank they'd usually dealt with had refused, but her father found a bank that had been willing to take the risk. Too late now. "Yes, well, he loved to take on new projects, and he was certain he had a winner."

Roger cleared his throat again. "So, what can I help you with, love?"

Though everyone had told her Ramirez Enterprises was invulnerable, she asked Roger if he knew of any weaknesses in Alejandro's company.

"I understand there may be some trouble in Dubai," Roger said. "Rumor has it they could lose the property they've sunk so much into. I have another client interested in property there, and they've heard rumblings."

Rebecca tapped her chin with a fingernail. "There *is* an accusation of impropriety in the permits process, right? Do you know anything about that?"

Roger sighed. "There's no evidence to support the charge thus far, but I know the man himself took the corporate jet over this morning. It must be something to get Ramirez to fly in."

He told her a few other things, about permits and engineers, architects, the Emir and a relative of some sort. Nothing specific, but things that could add up to trouble for a hotel chain trying to build a new resort. She'd fielded similar problems in the past, so understood both the import of the issues and the hassle of bureaucratic red tape.

"You'll let me know if you hear anything?" he finished.

"I'll keep my ears open." After what Alejandro had done to her, she refused to feel guilty about it. If there was even a remote chance she could wrest Layton International from him, she had to take it. Her father would have demanded no less.

An image of Alejandro talking about his daughter in the past tense sprang to mind. *No.* No room for weakness. This was business, not personal.

"I'd appreciate that," he replied. "We're digging, looking for an Achilles' heel, but so far there's nothing to report."

"Roger," Rebecca said, when they were wrapping up the conversation. "I wanted to ask you something else before you go."

"Shoot, love."

"Why'd you pull out of the Ramirez deal five years ago?"

He hesitated a moment before speaking. "We decided it wasn't a good investment after all."

"But you financed *our* South American acquisitions."

"The stake was less than Ramirez required."

Rebecca's temples throbbed. "But you didn't pull out of Ramirez because of us, right?"

He sighed. "Your father thought it was a bad bet, love, and he didn't want to do business with us if we took the risk. Ramirez had a reputation as a risk-taker, you see. He was unorthodox, and several of our investors were already wary. Your father's opinion simply helped put the nail in the coffin."

Rebecca's heart pinched. Yes, her father had been at the top of his game then. He'd had a lot of influence in the industry and would have been listened to with the reverence of an Oracle. She drew a breath into her painfully tight chest. "All right, thanks."

"Ring me if you hear anything about Dubai."

"I will."

They said their goodbyes, and Rebecca laid her cell phone on the desk before leaning back in her chair. Icy dread dripped down her spine. It just might be her fault that Alejandro had lost his backing after all.

Oh, God.

In a moment of weakness she'd called her mother when she'd been sitting in the Madrid airport five years ago, her eyes puffy and red, her throat sore. She'd had no one else to talk to. She'd been stunned, hurt, humiliated. She could still see the severe-looking wedding coordinator, with her folder and her samples, asking for the groom and saying, "*Gracias*, I will wait for him to return. His fiancée is anxious to begin the plans, yes?"

Ridiculously, she'd hoped for a mother-daughter connection, some sage advice. How she'd forgotten for those few moments that her mother was as shallow as a puddle, she'd never know. Amelie Layton had made sympathetic noises, but she'd spent more time talking to her dog than she had offering advice.

Later, Rebecca had realized she'd just needed to say it aloud to someone. Once she'd confessed, she'd had the good sense to regret it. She'd made her mother promise not to say anything to her father—a "just us girls" pact. After the incident with Parker Gaines—hired by her father to prove that she was a weak, vulnerable female—she didn't want to give him any further evidence of her "feminine weakness". She had to be strong, had to prove she could run Layton International someday.

Since it wasn't like her father to keep quiet about her personal life—especially something negative—she'd breathed a sigh of relief when he'd never said anything. Her mother, bless her, had kept the secret. Indeed, thinking back on it, her father's dislike of Alejandro seemed to have come later. Rebecca thought the explanation was simple rivalry; Ramirez Enterprises' influence and reach had grown while the Layton star was sinking. It'd been hard for her father to accept as the years went by and their positions were reversed.

Fury boiled over. She wanted the truth, no matter how difficult. She stabbed the number of her mother's cell phone.

"Did you tell Dad about Alejandro Ramirez?" she demanded, when Amelie Layton answered.

"Is that any way to talk to your mother, *ma belle*?" Amelie's voice trailed off as she shushed her dogs. "I may have. I can't remember."

CHAPTER FIVE

SEVERAL days of fighting with government officials had put Alejandro in a foul mood, especially since nothing was solved yet. Worse, his parents' anniversary party was tonight at the Villa de Musica. As much as he'd like to stay home and sit on the terrace with a glass of sherry, he had to put in an appearance.

The plane had landed half an hour ago. How his chauffeur had got them through the mess that was Madrid traffic and to his villa in that little amount of time was nothing short of a miracle. One of these days he would put in that helicopter pad he kept thinking about. As his business spread, so did the necessity for trips abroad.

He usually kept a tuxedo on the jet, along with several suits and other things he might need, but his personal assistant had somehow sent everything to the cleaners without first rotating in a fresh supply. He had barely an hour to change and be on his way to the hotel.

Alejandro ripped at his tie and tossed it on the bed. Señora Flores had laid out a fresh shirt for him, and his tux was hanging nearby, ready to go. Why must he suffer through these damnable parties every year? On the outside, Carmen and Juan Ramirez seemed the happy couple. They played it up quite well, in fact, except for a few public incidents Alejandro didn't like to recall in detail.

But Alejandro knew the truth. So did his sister, Valencia—which was why she always found an excuse to stay in Paris with her husband—and Roberto before he had died.

Juan enjoyed his various mistresses *du jour*, and Carmen enjoyed her society committees as well as a little too much wine. Still, it mostly worked for them, even if there were moments of drama. Carmen forcing a mistress out of Juan's city apartment naked, for instance. Juan cutting off Carmen's credit line the moment she went abroad on a shopping trip.

It was always something. As if Alejandro needed more confirmation that being chained to another person for life was bad. He'd tried it once—albeit without the drama and emotion—and that was enough. Emotionless or not, marriage wasn't for him. Sometimes he thought it might be nice to have more children, but his sister's children would inherit the business when it was time. He did not need to risk the heartbreak that marrying and having a child could bring ever again.

He finished inserting the studs into his shirt and sleeves and went to work on the tie. After three attempts he was ready to ring for Señora Flores—except this was her night off and she wasn't here.

Swearing, he grabbed his jacket and headed for the limo. The doors to the terrace were open as he passed through the Great Room. A female voice drifted to his ears and he changed direction. Something kicked him low in the gut when he emerged onto the terrace and saw her. It should surprise him, the physical jolt, but it didn't. Not any longer, and not since he'd decided to do something about it.

Rebecca sat at the broad table under the arbor, the last rays of sunlight turning her hair to molten gold. She had her computer open, a pen in her mouth, and a cell phone to her ear. She did not hear him approach, so he took time to study her profile. Her golden hair was unadorned, falling to a point just below her shoulders in soft waves. She'd tucked it behind her ear, and a small diamond winked in her lobe. Her legs were crossed at the ankles as she leaned forward, concentrating on her screen and on the person on the other end of the phone. She wore a short tropical-print skirt. He let his gaze caress the length of those long legs before traveling up her body, over the white tank top molding her breasts, coming to rest on her face.

He was going to enjoy taking her to bed. His groin tightened in anticipation, his body remembering how it'd been with her all those years ago.

Dios, in spite of everything she fired his blood, made him burn to possess her.

"Do you have those projections?" she said to the person on the other end, and a jolt of awareness shot through him. He'd once had a liaison with an accountant, but his usual companions were actresses or models or idle heiresses. Rebecca, for all her pampering, knew her way around the business world. He liked that about her.

Oh, yes, he'd made the right decision. He was going to thoroughly enjoy her before his revenge was complete.

She glanced sideways, her eyes widening when she saw him.

"Yes, thanks, John. Get me those numbers as soon as you can. I'll talk to you later." She set the phone down and offered him a wary smile. "How was your trip?"

"Tiring," he said. He held the tie up. "Can you fix this?"

He thought vaguely that he ought to hate asking her, that he was merely confirming her opinion he was more suited to a bullring than a boardroom, but he was too irritated at the prospect of the party to care.

If he'd expected a superior look from the spoiled woman sitting in his courtyard, he didn't get it.

"I can try," she said, standing, biting her lip between her teeth as she took the tie and slipped it around his neck. Her fingers were cool where they brushed his skin, and yet a spark of awareness lingered where she'd touched. Her sweet scent stole into his nostrils. He couldn't understand why, of all the women in the world, he currently wanted this one. But he intended to have her. Now that he'd decided bedding her fit into his plans, there was no need to wait. Tonight, one way or the other, she would be his.

Awareness of her crept through him, made him hard. What would she think if she realized he was on the edge of burying himself inside her?

Her gaze never wavered from his throat as she worked, almost as if she feared what she might see if she looked up at him. *Sí, be afraid of me, amor. I intend to possess you, to ruin you. You are finished and don't even know it.*

"Did you miss me?" he teased, his sensual tone at odds with his dark thoughts.

Her brows shot up, her expression a strange mixture of disbelief and—was it guilt? Interesting. He filed it away for future contemplation.

"You're kidding, right?" Her voice broke at the last. She refocused on his tie, twisting and tugging.

Alejandro pressed his advantage. "Perhaps I am not. Did you not enjoy our time together in the pool, *bella*?"

She yanked the tie too tight, nearly choking him, then jerked it loose and swore before trying again. "I've forgotten all about it," she said. "It didn't mean a thing."

Her red face and clumsy fingers told him differently.

"I wanted to taste you," he said, just to see what she would do. "To lay you back and dip my tongue into your sweetness. Are you still sweet, Rebecca?"

Her chest heaved, once. She bent her head lower, her lip undergoing punishment from her teeth as she concentrated. He wanted to suck that lip between his own, make love to it until she was pliant, begging him to move on to another delicious part of her.

How could he want this woman he hated? He didn't know,

but *maldito sea*, since he'd freed himself to do so he could think of almost nothing else.

She tugged the tie and stepped back with a triumphant expression. "There—all done."

He touched the knot, tested it for tightness. *"Gracias."* Then he closed the distance between them, giving her no quarter. It was not in his nature to prevaricate once he'd decided he wanted something. "Would you like that, *querida*? Would you like me to taste you?"

She made a choked sound, slipped past him and fiddled with the briefcase she'd left open on the table. "Stop, I don't want to hear it."

"Are you certain? Imagine it…imagine the ecstasy."

Her eyes closed. "No."

"Do you remember the first time?"

He thought she wouldn't respond, but she nodded—just a quick dip of her chin.

"It could be like that again." *Dios*, he wanted it. Right now, this second, he wanted it to be that way just once more. To forget why he had to hate her, why he had to destroy her. To just feel the good things again.

She snapped her laptop closed and stuffed it into her briefcase before glaring at him with fiery blue eyes. "That's impossible, Alejandro. The first time we were together, I stupidly thought I was the only woman in your life. You let me find out in the most humiliating way possible that I wasn't the only one—or even the primary one."

He recognized that she needed to cloak herself in her mantle of righteous anger so she wouldn't feel the pull of desire between them. But he did not intend to allow her that comfort. "Anyone can hire a wedding planner, Rebecca. That particular one was hired by my father, with the express purpose of chasing you away and pushing me into a marriage I had not agreed to."

She looked a bit shocked—and very doubtful. "Why should I believe you? And why, if that's the case, didn't you tell me five years ago?"

His laugh was bitter. He snapped it off in midstream and pinned her with a hard stare. "Because you were a coward. You ran away like a petulant child. What was I to do? Chase you back to New York and force you to listen to me?"

Rebecca's heart skipped a beat. This was not what she'd expected tonight. She'd been working with her chief financial officer on some projections for the Kai Lani chain of resorts, and fielding calls from her human resources director about Ramirez's plans and how it would affect jobs. Except she didn't yet know what Alejandro had in mind, so she'd had to put the woman off with vague platitudes about the future. Which had angered and frustrated her. And reminded her how precarious her position was.

She hadn't expected Alejandro to return in the midst of it all, and she certainly hadn't expected *this*. A discussion of their painful past was the last thing she'd have thought was possible tonight. Yet here he was, telling her it was his father who'd sent the wedding planner and that it had been deliberate.

She could hardly wrap her mind around it. Worse, she feared he was right in at least one respect: she'd run away because she couldn't take it, because she'd already shown poor judgment once before. She hadn't trusted herself to make a sound decision. She'd needed distance, time, space to think.

She'd got her time, and plenty of it, hadn't she? "You should have made me understand," she forced from her dry throat. Could it possibly be true that his family had wanted to manipulate him into the wedding? That his father would have done such a thing?

Why not? Her own father had gone to extraordinary

lengths, hiring Parker to insinuate himself into her life, hadn't he? And all to prove a point to her. A painful point about her own vulnerability and neediness. Rebecca shivered as she stared at Alejandro. He was fully capable of lying to her in order to make her feel worse than she already did about what had happened between them.

He stood before her, devilishly dark and deliciously handsome in his custom-fit tuxedo. His skin had darkened beneath the hot Arabian sun over the last few days, setting off the lightning-silver of his eyes. Eyes that speared her with scorn.

"Perhaps you should have *trusted* me," he bit out. A second later, he raked a hand through his dark hair, swore in Spanish. "As if it would have mattered. No, your plan was always to ruin me, to take what you could and destroy Ramirez Enterprises in the process. You nearly succeeded."

Her throat ached with denials. But what was the point? Though her mother couldn't say definitively whether or not she'd told Rebecca's father about the aborted affair, it was still Jackson Layton's threat to take his business elsewhere that had cost Alejandro the deal he'd worked so hard to procure. Like it or not, the Laytons *were* responsible.

But she could defend *her* motives without hesitation. "You haven't proved anything to me, Alejandro. My only plan when I came to the Villa de Musica was to see the restoration. I didn't plan to meet you, and I certainly didn't plan to fall in love with you. It would have been so much easier if I'd never met you."

Wasn't that the truth? Five long years, and she'd never really succeeded in forgetting him. Before he'd summoned her to Madrid she'd still been blissfully able to deceive herself that the years had done their work. But she hadn't forgotten after all, and every day she spent with him only made the memories more painful.

"Yes, it is hard to look a man in the eye before you cut him down," he said, more to himself than to her, glancing at his watch. "I have no time for this now, but be assured I have no need to lie. It matters not whether you believe me."

"Then why did you say it?" she said, her throat tight. What if he was telling her the truth? What if she'd been as mistaken about his engagement as he had about her motives?

He shrugged. "Because I am tired of your self-righteousness."

Rebecca blinked. "Self-righteousness?" Who was he kidding? He was the most self-righteous man on the planet. She snatched up the folder she'd been working on. She couldn't deal with this right now. "I'm going inside now. Have a nice time."

Alejandro caught her arm as she turned away. "You're coming with me."

"What? Where?" she stammered. He was wearing a tuxedo, not a casual pair of trousers and a shirt. Wherever he was going, she couldn't show up in a tank top and wispy skirt. "I have work to do. I can't go with you."

"This is not a request, Rebecca. You will come. Now."

"I don't have anything suitable to wear," she said, thrusting her chin up and stating the obvious. Or the not so obvious if the way he looked at her was any indication.

"There is a boutique in the hotel. You will buy a dress. Now, come—we are out of time."

"But, Alejandro, really—"

"Need I remind you I am the one in control here?" he ground out, slamming the door on her protest. "You have no choice, Rebecca."

She gripped her briefcase, her knuckles whitening. She had an urge to close her eyes and count to a hundred before speaking, the way her mother had used to make her do when she was upset and crying over something. It had worked to calm her down when she was ten, though it had also made her feel unimportant and unloved.

Ah, but you are unloved. This man does not love you, never did. Never could and never will.

She concentrated on his cold, handsome features. Not that she wanted him to love her now. No, that desire was in the past. This man was nothing like the Alejandro she'd once loved.

But he's still inside there.

No.

She closed the door firmly on such thoughts. "Very well," she said, as coolly as she could manage given the erratic beating of her heart. "If you will allow me to drop these things in my room?"

His nod was brief. Arrogant and sure. She itched to smack him. Instead, she put her things away and returned to join him beside the limousine waiting out front. He held the door open for her, then followed her inside. A moment later they were being whisked through the darkening streets of Madrid.

"We're going where?" Rebecca's heart climbed into her throat, thrumming in panic. His parents' anniversary party? But *why*? She closed her eyes, swallowed. *Oh, God.* She'd never met his parents—had, in fact, no idea what his relationship with them was like. He'd spoken of a brother and sister, she remembered that much. His brother had died tragically only a few months before she'd met Alejandro. He'd never talked of it, and she hadn't asked because their relationship had been so new.

But would his parents know who *she* was? That she was the woman he'd been sleeping with while he was engaged to someone else? How could she possibly show up at their special party tonight and hold her head up?

Alejandro glanced up from his PDA, his expression showing he hadn't missed the note of alarm threading through her voice. "The party is a grand affair, Rebecca. No one will notice another guest. Besides, I am the one paying for it."

It was true she'd envisioned some sort of small, lavish dinner party instead of a "grand affair", but the idea of several hundred people at this event did nothing to quell her uneasiness. His parents would still be there, and if she were with Alejandro she'd still have to meet them. Perhaps that was his plan: *Mom, Dad, meet Rebecca Layton—the slut who stole my deal and tried to ruin me five years ago.*

But that wasn't the source of her deepest anxiety. No, if she were brutally honest with herself, most of her unease was brought on by the proximity of the man sitting across from her, his legs sprawled casually to either side of hers. Long lashes shadowed his eyes as he concentrated on the screen of his PDA. Tanned fingers manipulated the keys deftly, sending and receiving information at the touch of a few buttons.

He'd talked of tasting her. She'd thought of almost nothing else since.

Memories of long ago crashed into her mind with alarming regularity. Sexual memories. Of Alejandro's skin against hers, of his hot tongue slicking a path down her body, finding her—

Rebecca pressed two fingers to her temples, willing the erotic images out of her head. She had to focus, had to prepare herself for whatever she would find at this party. Maybe no one would notice her—or maybe it really was another facet of Alejandro's plan to humiliate her in front of as many people as possible. Why else had he ordered her to come with him?

He couldn't know how tormented she was, simply looking at him, how part of her wanted to reach out and find the man he used to be beneath the hard exterior. How she ached to touch his smooth skin, to trace her fingers along the seam of his lips, to breathe in the warm scent of him the way she'd once done. To see him actually smile at her with warmth.

Stop, just stop. He hates you.

When the limousine pulled into the circular drive of the

Villa de Musica, Rebecca wanted to melt into the plush leather seat. A horde of photographers clustered together near the entrance, snapping away as people emerged from the cars that crawled in a steady stream through the driveway.

She wiped clammy palms down her skirt, tried to straighten it out as best as possible. What would she look like beside Alejandro in the papers, dressed like a beach bum?

Alejandro slipped his phone into his pocket and frowned at her. "There is nothing to be afraid of," he said.

She tilted her chin up, reached down deep for her inner socialite. Her mother would expect nothing less than total poise, regardless of the situation. "I'm not afraid. I'm just not prepared. You gave me no warning."

"Sometimes the best things in life are spontaneous, yes?"

She wasn't sure if he was joking or needling her. The car ahead of them disgorged its passengers. A woman stopped and posed, tossing long dark hair over her shoulders and tilting her hips from side to side. Flashes burst into life, lighting the entry as if it had been pitch-black before.

Alejandro swore. He stabbed the intercom button and snapped out an order in Spanish. The limo didn't stop when their turn came but continued through the drive and out to the street.

"I forgot about the paparazzi. We'll use the back entrance."

"Won't a few of them be stationed back there for just that purpose?"

He shrugged. "*Sí*, but my security is very thorough."

Rebecca let out her breath. "Thank you," she said.

"It is not for you," he said curtly. "I have no wish to answer questions tonight."

She crossed her arms and willed away the stab of hurt. Of course he hadn't ordered the car to go around to the back in order to spare her any embarrassment. Was she an idiot? No, the more pain he could cause her, the better. Worse, she actually understood it. If her father hadn't pressured Roger into backing out of the deal, what else might Alejandro have accomplished?

Rebecca studied the hotel as they snaked around behind it. The Villa de Musica was one of the grander buildings in Madrid. It had once belonged to a famous opera singer. It had been sold over the years, falling into a state of shabby decline before being rescued by Alejandro and restored to its glory days. She hadn't been inside since she'd left his suite five years ago.

How would she feel walking inside, remembering? She would soon find out.

The limo slipped behind a security barrier. Moments later someone popped open the door and they rushed into a small service entrance at the rear of the hotel.

The hall was narrow, and she had no choice but to follow Alejandro as he worked his way through the labyrinth. He ushered her into an elevator. A minute later the doors slid open and they were hurrying down another hall. Alejandro stopped and keyed in a code on a pad beside a door. So he'd gone high-tech in the last five years. Interesting.

Rebecca stumbled to a halt behind him as the door swung open. *The* suite. The one he'd lived in five years ago, because he'd sunk everything he had into the hotel. It wasn't the first place they had made love, but it was the location where she'd felt like she'd shared a home with him. She'd been staying in the luxurious private suite on the top floor, with its own pool and rooftop terrace, but this suite was smaller, more private, and they'd retreated here often. Eventually she had checked out of her room and moved into his.

"I'll have one of the saleswomen bring up some things," Alejandro said, pulling out his phone. "You can get dressed and come downstairs when you're ready."

She dragged her gaze from the door to the bedroom, forced

herself to focus on what he was saying. To breathe normally. *In. Out. In. Out.*

"Fine," she said evenly, determined not to let him see how affected she was by being back in this room with him. She managed to stroll over to the couch, sink down on it and cross her legs casually.

He finished calling the boutique, then turned to her. His mouth snapped shut, whatever he was about to say forgotten. He usually moved with the easy grace of a panther, but now he took a halting step forward. Stopped. Shook his head and scrubbed a hand through his dark hair.

She started to ask him what was wrong, but a memory hurtled into her brain and her mouth went slack. This couch. Him. The two of them. Nothing between them but sweat, passionate words, breathy moans.

The heat in his gaze told her he was remembering it too. It shocked her, the raw primal urge she saw in his face, and it compelled her. She wanted him. Oh, God, how she wanted him. The only time she'd ever felt truly cherished was with him. It was everything she could do not to rise, go to him, pull his head down to hers. Try to recapture that feeling.

She closed her eyes, swallowed. Willed the memory away: the scents, tastes and sounds of it. It was too real, too painful.

The door clicked quietly and her eyes shot open. But there was no saleswoman arriving with dresses. The room was empty and she was alone.

CHAPTER SIX

WHAT was wrong with him? Why had he fled the suite like a
bull was shadowing his heels, running him to ground? He'd
stayed there dozens of times since she'd left. Hundreds of
times. He'd even taken other women to bed there, in an effort
to erase her from his memory. He'd been positive he'd done
it too—until he'd turned around and seen her on the couch.

He should have left her in the villa and ignored the dark
demon urging him to bring her along tonight. It would have
been easier. And made more sense.

Alejandro stalked into the hotel offices and went over some
paperwork the manager had been asking him to approve. But
he kept seeing Rebecca, her arms crossed beneath her breasts,
her legs so long and bare in her little skirt. Superimposed over
the picture of her sitting there tonight was a picture of her on
the same couch, beneath him, naked and writhing and
begging.

Madre de Dios, how much could a man take?

*"Alejandro, please, I love you. Please, before I die. Please,
please, please, I need you…"*

He'd obliged her, of course, but not before making them
both crazy with need. What would have happened had he done
what he wanted tonight? Had he walked over there and
stripped her naked? Would he be lost in her right now?

Sí, without a doubt.

He shouldn't have brought her up here. It hadn't been his plan. Until the flashbulbs had gone off and he had registered the alarm on Rebecca's face. He didn't know why he'd felt compelled to order the driver to the back, but he'd done it before thinking about it. He should have let her face the cameras in her casual clothes, let her feel the embarrassment. Except it was his doing she was here tonight, and he'd felt obligated to protect her.

He grabbed a pen and signed off on the paperwork. After he left the office, it took him nearly three quarters of an hour to get to the ballroom because he kept running into people who needed his time or attention. A cabinet minister, a senior-ranking diplomat, a wealthy diamond merchant, an actress he'd once bedded—the last was particularly difficult to extract himself from. She was beautiful, sleek and expensive, in a sheer designer gown that left no doubt about the assets underneath the material—and she left him completely cold.

He needed to find Rebecca. He was starting to feel just a little bit guilty he'd stayed away so long. She would have had to enter the packed room alone, not knowing anyone and not speaking the language. Of course nearly everyone also spoke English these days, so she would not find it difficult to converse. But he should have been with her nevertheless. Easing her into this situation didn't mean he was going soft, or that he was giving up his plans for her. On the contrary, the more relaxed he made her, the more devastating it would be when he threw her out with nothing.

He accepted a glass of champagne from a tray and idly surveyed the crowd. His mother stood near the bar, surrounded by women. He went over to give her a kiss.

"Alejandro, my love! I feared you would not make it back in time."

"I would never miss your party, *Madre*."

Carmen Ramirez pursed her lips. "Unlike Valencia. She canceled yet again—can you believe it?"

"Where is Father?" Alejandro asked, unwilling to indulge a mini-tantrum against his sister for even a second. He understood why Valencia canceled each year. His presence would have to be enough for them both. Thankfully, Valencia had finally given up apologizing to him for making him bear the burden alone.

Carmen waved a bejeweled hand as she took a sip of champagne. "He has found a woman to dance with, I believe."

At that moment the crowd parted, clearing a path to the floor. Juan Ramirez embraced a sleek woman in a shimmering midnight-blue gown, staring down at her with such intent that Alejandro decided to intervene before the evening digressed into a very public Ramirez family drama.

He excused himself from his mother, who had already turned back to her friends, and threaded his way through the guests. Juan swayed back and forth, his attention solely on the woman in his arms.

Her back was to Alejandro, but he had to acknowledge that if her front was as enticing as her back he couldn't blame Juan for his interest. Blonde hair was swept into a pile on her head, revealing a slender neck, bare shoulders and a plunging dress that stopped just short of the curve of her buttocks. Long legs seemed to go on forever, accentuated by four-inch heels.

Interest stirred, surprising him. And relieving him. So he *could* feel desire for a woman other than Rebecca Layton. *Gracias, Dios.* When he tired of her, it would be simple to move on to someone else.

But right now it was his father's interest that most concerned him. Juan's hand rested on the smooth flesh of the woman's back, its darkness in contrast to the pearlescent sheen of her skin.

Ten more minutes and Alejandro would have been too late. Juan would have whisked her away to somewhere more private, party and wife be damned. His father looked up, frowning when he caught sight of Alejandro. He bent to say something in the delicate shell of the woman's ear. She stopped moving to the music, turned as if startled.

Alejandro stumbled to a halt as her blue eyes collided with his. Shock, fury and lust blazed to life all at once, roaring up inside him like an inferno. One word echoed through his brain: *mine.*

He closed the distance between them and yanked her from his father's lecherous fingers. He barely registered the gasps around them as she stumbled into him. He caught her around the waist, steadying her. His fingertips brushed the warm silky skin of her exposed back. Inexplicable fury coursed though him and he aimed it at the easiest target.

"Attempting to buy another hotel with your body, Rebecca?" he grated, as much to mask the force of his desire as to hurt her for making him want her like this. Without *reason*, without *sense.*

She jerked away from him, her expression caving. "You bastard!" she whispered fiercely.

"Alejandro, you will apologize to the lady," his father said, disapproval drawing his brows together in sharp slashes. "Your mother would be ashamed."

Before he could speak, Rebecca turned to his father and smiled. The corners of her mouth wavered. "Thank you, Señor Ramirez, but it's not necessary. Your son and I are old enemies, I'm afraid. We hurl words like daggers."

"But this is no way to treat one's guest," Juan insisted. "My son was not raised this way, *señorita.* I apologize for his rudeness."

She refused to look at him as she spoke to his father. "I'm afraid I bring out the worst in him."

His father looked aghast. "Alejandro, how is this possible? This lady is so charming, so lovely—"

"As are all ladies to you, Father." *Maldito sea*, the old reprobate was unbelievable. "I think Mother is near the bar. Since it is your anniversary, perhaps you should ask *her* for a dance."

Juan looked as if he would argue, but he finally nodded. "*Sí*, you are correct. Dear lady," he continued, taking Rebecca's hand and kissing it, "I hope you will enjoy yourself at our party tonight. We shall see you at our table for the toast, yes?"

"*Gracias*," Rebecca said. "I would be honored."

The band began to play a new song as Juan walked away. Before Rebecca could escape, Alejandro pulled her into his arms. The people who'd stopped to listen began to mingle again.

"Don't touch me," she said. "Just let me go and I'll leave."

"You won't," he said, drawing her in close, fitting her against his body. She felt so good against him. Smelled good. He concentrated on tempering his body's reaction to her. *Later.* "The night is far from over."

Her palms rested on his chest, but she refused to meet his eyes. Instead, she studied his shirtfront. "I get it, Alejandro. You wanted to humiliate me by bringing me here tonight. Now that you've succeeded just let me go. I've had enough."

He hadn't brought her for that reason, but there was no sense in denying it. She would not believe him. And what could he tell her anyway? That he'd brought her with him because he'd had an impulse to do so? "How did you end up dancing with my father?"

Her lashes lifted, and he was momentarily stunned by the sheen of moisture in her eyes. She blinked and looked away again. "He looks like you. I introduced myself and asked where I could find you. He said he would take me to you, but we ended up here."

Yes, he didn't doubt it for a moment. His father could not resist a beautiful woman.

"But then, of course," she continued with a half-choked laugh, "I realized that I could implement my diabolical plan to sleep my way to another hotel. I was just about to claim my victim when you intervened. I'm sure I could have gotten several hotels out of him, assuming he owns a single one."

Alejandro blew out a breath. For once he had been wrong about her. But just this once. "I should not have said that."

She didn't look at him. "You shouldn't have, but you'd do it again in a heartbeat. You insist on believing the worst about me."

It was true. Part of him always wanted to stomp on her spirit. He wanted to grind her beneath his heels, make her feel every moment of every day how wrong she'd been to steal from him. She'd forced him into a choice he should have never made, *would* never have made if she hadn't left and ripped away whatever happiness he'd felt with her.

And yet he was drawn to her. Could still feel sympathy for her. It was a paradox he didn't understand. "We will not talk about this tonight," he declared. He didn't want to think too deeply about his feelings for this woman right now. He wanted to savor her body, that was all. No feelings, no past. Just heat and passion and the sweetness of release.

Her laugh was bitter. "No, of course not. God forbid that you might actually be forced to rethink your opinion of me. I wasn't seducing your father, but naturally the same can't be said of how far I will go with you, right? And you'll allow nothing to contradict that opinion, so we won't even discuss it."

"What could you possibly say to change my mind?" he bit out. "There is nothing you can say, no proof you can offer, that changes what you did to me."

Her throat moved as she swallowed. "No, I can't prove my innocence," she said softly, her voice heavy with emotion.

People began to clap politely. It took a moment before

Alejandro realized the music had stopped. But he and Rebecca were still locked tightly together, their gazes tangled. Hers was sad, beseeching—disappointed?

He stepped back as if she were a live wire, forced his hands to his sides. "You cannot prove it because you are guilty, Rebecca. Cease trying to make me doubt what I know to be true. It will not work. We can never go back to those days before you betrayed me."

Rebecca sipped champagne and chatted with a woman who was the wife of a Spanish television star. But her attention wasn't on the woman as much as it was on the man across from her. Alejandro was so achingly handsome it hurt. And so remote it chilled her.

From the moment they'd left the dance floor and come to the head table he'd been closed off and cold. Of course he would never believe she hadn't been the one to betray him. She knew that. But being here now, in the place where she'd shared so much with him, her emotions were skewed and raw.

From the moment he'd left her in the suite she'd been on edge. She felt like an exposed nerve, reacting to every stimulus, aching with pain, wanting to escape. She'd actually hoped to see approval in his eyes when he'd first seen her at the party. The dress she'd chosen from the few the salesgirl had brought fit like it was custom-designed for her. The shoes were exquisite. A quick visit from one of the salon's stylists, and her hair and makeup were perfect. Looking at herself in the mirror, she'd never have believed that a half hour before she'd been more suited for an evening by the beach rather than a formal gathering at a posh hotel.

She'd swallowed her trepidation and gone downstairs, but Alejandro had been nowhere to be found. Seeing Juan Ramirez had been a relief. The man was a carbon copy of his son—just older and more distinguished-looking. He'd shown no signs of recognizing her name when she had introduced herself. She'd believed he would whisk her to Alejandro. It was only after he'd pulled her into his arms and started swaying that she realized she'd been deceived, that Juan was a bit of a Casanova. Rather than be impolite, she'd danced. And of course Alejandro had chosen that moment to appear. The universe had a bizarre sense of humor.

Now Alejandro sat beside his mother, listening politely while she talked about something Rebecca couldn't understand. *Complained* about something, more likely, judging from the expression on her face and the speed with which she spoke. Her champagne sloshed over the rim of the glass she clutched; she didn't seem to notice. Alejandro calmly took it and put it down, away from her. A moment later she flagged down a waiter and snagged a fresh glass.

Rebecca didn't miss the frown Alejandro gave his mother as she quaffed most of the liquid in one go. Juan Ramirez chose that moment to appear, and Carmen shot up out of her seat. She would have fallen down again had Alejandro not bolted up and steadied her.

The table grew quiet as Carmen railed at her husband. Rebecca might not understand Spanish, but she could tell the conversation wasn't a pleasant one. Juan refused to look at her. A second later she lunged. Alejandro stopped her, caught her close as she began to sob. Juan pushed his son out of the way and put his arms around his wife. Oddly enough, Carmen didn't shove him away. She clutched his lapels and buried her face against his chest, her shoulders shaking as she cried.

Alejandro sank into his chair, a stony expression on his face.

The woman beside Rebecca whispered, "My husband tells me that Señor Ramirez has been seeing Isabella Ayala. She is a young actress, very promising."

Rebecca blinked at the woman, her heart slowing to a crawl in her chest.

"No, no." She patted Rebecca's hand. "Juan—not Alejandro, darling. It is clear that Alejandro is smitten with you, though it is too bad about his parents." She tsked. "This one is far more serious than usual, though. He may even leave her for this woman. Or so my husband says. I am not so sure, however."

A few moments later Rebecca murmured an excuse and rose from her chair. Alejandro's face was frozen in a blank mask as he watched his parents. He glanced over at her and she offered him a sympathetic smile. His expression didn't change.

She hurried to the ladies' room, needing to be alone for a minute or two. She just wanted to sit and breathe and be surrounded by muted noise rather than this discordant mix of voices, clanging dishes and music. She wanted to think without watching Alejandro and wondering at every turn what he was feeling inside.

Rebecca sank onto one of the plush benches and gazed at her reflection. Her table companion, whose name she'd forgotten almost as soon as they were introduced, had been wrong, or was just being nice, about Alejandro being smitten with her. But her heart ached at the look of helplessness on his face while he dealt with his parents. Oh, he masked it well, but she saw the pain and anger he tried to hide.

She didn't *want* to feel sympathy for him. She simply couldn't afford it. She had to be hard, cold, ruthless—just like him. Layton International depended on it.

Rebecca touched up her lipstick, smoothed her dress, and returned to the party. Alejandro's parents were gone now, but Alejandro stood with a strikingly beautiful woman, his hand on her arm, his head bent close to hers as he talked. Her face seemed a little tight as she took a step away and disappeared into the crowd. Not a romantic moment, then. Rebecca didn't want to analyze the relief that washed through her at the realization.

Alejandro whirled, catching sight of her. He came and took her arm, tucked it into his. "We're going now," he said in clipped tones.

"Fine with me," she replied, her pulse thumping. She didn't like seeing him this way, didn't like the way his emotions played over his face in the rare moments when he struggled for control. It forced her to see him as human and vulnerable, reminded her that she'd once loved him with every last breath in her body.

They left the hotel by the front entrance this time. The paparazzi snapped photos and called out to him, but he ignored them. Soon they were in the car, moving down the drive and out into the *paseo*. The silence crushed down on her until she had to speak.

"The hotel is even better than I remembered," she said.

"Gracias."

"The service is impeccable."

"Sí."

Rebecca sighed. There was only one thing she could say. "I'm sorry, Alejandro."

He turned his head. She was looking out the window, her arms folded beneath her breasts, the material of her dress softly shimmering in the light leaking into the car. The fabric skimmed her curves like a lover, clung to all the peaks and hollows he wanted to explore.

"What are you sorry for, Rebecca?"

Her eyes met his, huge blue pools in her beautiful face. Her throat moved as she swallowed. "What happened. Your parents."

He was too weary to try and put a positive spin on it. "They do what they do," he said. "It has always been so."

"Is it true?" she said. "About the actress, I mean."

"It was," he replied. "But no longer."

"That was her you were talking to, wasn't it?"

He sighed. "*Sí*. But she will not get what she wants. I will ruin her first." He'd warned Isabella Ayala what he would do if he ever heard of her with his father again. Juan would find another mistress—he always did—and Carmen would accept it readily enough. But Isabella was angling for a ring, for wealth and position. He'd set her straight. Without him, his parents had no money of their own. And he would not hesitate to cut his father off without a euro should Isabella succeed in her quest.

"Do you ever get tired, Alejandro?"

"*¿Qué?*" He came back to himself with a start, focused on the woman across from him.

She leaned across the seat and put her hands on his knees. The warmth of her palms through the fabric of his trousers stunned him. The drumbeat of desire flared to life in his blood. *Dios*, he couldn't even remember the question she'd asked him. If she were to run those palms up to his groin, he'd be a very happy man.

Her soft voice brought him back to the moment. "It must be very tiring, seeing the world in black and white, ruining people right and left. It's okay to see shades of gray, you know, to not always need to control everything. The world will still go around. You don't have to make it move."

Something knifed into his heart. She pushed herself back, breaking that electric contact, and he found himself staring at her. Since he was a boy, he'd always needed to be in control, to order his world as best he could. Control was his security blanket.

"You know nothing of it," he snapped. "I have always had to be responsible, to take care of myself and my family. Control is everything."

She looked sad. "It's not the only thing."

He sliced a hand through the air, dismissing her. "*Sí*, it is everything. My parents have never understood the need for control either. Did you not notice this tonight?"

She bowed her head. "I understand you might have been embarrassed, but—"

"Embarrassed?" He laughed harshly. "*Dios*, if only it were that simple. No, those two have always subjected me—and Roberto and Valencia—to their tantrums, their rages, their personal dramas. If I hadn't found the control they lacked within myself, I would not be who I am today."

He pinched the bridge of his nose. "Roberto died because he had no strength. He was just like my parents in his own way, and he paid the price. Valencia married her Parisian and rarely returns to Spain."

"I didn't know," she said softly.

She watched him with those sympathetic eyes, and he found himself teetering on the edge. How had she seen so deeply into him? Or was it simply a coincidence?

A sudden need to lash out at her, to inflict pain, overtook him.

He spoke with scorn. "We cannot all have a privileged life like yours, Rebecca. Some of us have to work very hard to succeed."

She choked out a laugh. "Oh, God, you think you know everything, don't you?" Her blue gaze flashed. "Well, you *don't*. So don't presume to tell me how I've lived my life."

"I know that you had a fortune handed to you on a silver platter. And that you and your father mismanaged everything so badly you leveraged your company to the hilt. If you hadn't been quite so greedy we would not be sitting here now."

She glared at him. "You're a fine one to talk of greed. With all you have at your fingertips, you still couldn't resist taking my company away, could you? Don't be hypocritical with *me*, Alejandro."

Finally, this was territory he understood. He almost laughed in relief. How easy it was to shift the conversation onto things he knew, things that didn't strip him bare and threaten to expose his soul to her gaze. "It's business, Rebecca."

"And it's personal," she shot back. "You came after us and didn't stop until you found a weakness."

For a moment he thought she was talking about what he'd done to put Layton International into jeopardy, but he realized she didn't know. If she did, she'd probably launch herself at him the way his mother had tried to attack his father tonight.

He almost told her. Almost explained that he owned the bank that had made the loans when no one else would, how he'd dangled the Thailand properties in front of their noses and waited for them to take the leap into debt in the first place. But something stopped him. Now wasn't the time. He wanted to savor his revenge first, wanted to take her down even farther than he already had.

Wanted her to need him, to beg for his touch the way she once had. She might have been lying about her love for him, but some of that physical need was real. He knew it now, knew it the second he'd turned and seen her on that couch. She'd remembered, the same as he had. Her jaw had gone slack, her eyes had glazed, and he'd known what she saw because he saw it too. It was why he'd had to get out.

"It was business first," he said coolly. "Layton International was no longer relevant. You need me to keep you viable in today's marketplace."

"You?" She shifted forward on the seat, her eyes glittering with sudden anger. "What do you know about relevancy, Alejandro? Until a few years ago you were *no one* in this industry! What you know about this business could fill a thimble compared to what my father knew, what he taught me—"

"Oh, yes," he ground out. "Your precious father, who sent *you* to do his dirty work instead of facing me like a man. Spare me your analysis, Rebecca. I'm still the one in control of Layton International."

He thought she would say something else, would let her true colors show now that she'd pointed out his inferior past, but she drew in a shaky breath and fixed her gaze on a point outside the window. The car had been crawling forward for some time. Now, it drew to a halt in the Puerta del Sol. Alejandro swore. Women with placards marched and shouted, blocking the square that was the heart of Old Madrid. Protests were common here, and there was nothing to do but wait as the *policía* directed cars down the side streets.

"I have a life. I'd like to get back to it," Rebecca said after they'd sat in silence for nearly ten minutes. "So if you plan to fire me, why don't you just get it over with and put us both out of our misery."

"Layton International *is* your life," he said.

She bristled. "I have an apartment, friends. I can't stay here forever, wondering what your plans are."

He was in no mood to be delicate with her. "You don't even have a pet fish, Rebecca. You have nothing in your life but work."

Her mouth dropped open as she looked at him. She snapped it shut. "How do you know I don't have a cat or a dog? A boyfriend?"

"I know that you eat Chinese takeout from a restaurant called Tai Pan on Friday nights when you are in town, that you buy flowers from a place called Robertson's, and that you have a grocery store across the street from your apartment but rarely visit it."

His investigators had been very thorough, though they hadn't been able to tell him everything. Like when she'd last spent the night with a man. He wanted to know, but he'd steadfastly refused to ask for that kind of information. It would show a level of interest in her life he no longer had.

All he really needed to know was that she had no long-term entanglements.

He watched as shock and hurt chased each other across her face. Now, why did the hurt pierce his conscience?

"You had me watched?"

He shrugged. "I am very thorough when taking over a company."   .

It was several moments before she spoke. "Oh, God, I can't believe..." She clasped her arms around her waist, her chest rising and falling faster and faster. "You...spied...on me. You—"

She bent double, air whistling in and out of her body as she took deep breaths.

Alarm snaked across his nerve endings, prickled the hair on his arms and neck. Of all the things he'd expected her to say or do, this hadn't crossed his mind as a possibility. "*Querida*, what is wrong?"

She didn't answer, just kept breathing hard. She was on the verge of hyperventilating and they were stuck in the Puerta del Sol. *Dios*, he felt so helpless. Like the night Anya—

No. He had to do something, *now*.

"Rebecca, hold on," he said, reaching for the door. "Just hold on." He had to get help—had to get one of the *policía* to radio for an ambulance. He could call, but the police would be faster.

"I have to get out of here," she wheezed. "Have to...go."

Before he could stop her, she reached for the opposite door and slipped out into the churning crowd.

CHAPTER SEVEN

ALREADY she could breathe again. Rebecca hugged herself tighter and forged through the crowd. She'd forgotten her wrap, but she wasn't going back. He'd had her *watched*. Investigated. Her privacy invaded. What else did he know? That she hadn't had sex in a year and a half? That she'd kept on taking birth control pills in the pitiful belief she might someday find a man she could love the way she'd once loved him?

It was pathetic. *She* was pathetic. She swiped at her cheeks, ignored the catcalls and whistles of the men she passed. She was vaguely familiar with the Puerta del Sol, but not enough to understand where it was in relation to anything else. She knew there was a department store on one side, El Corte Inglés, but that was in the direction of the protestors, who now congregated around the statue of a Spanish king on a horse. To one end of the square was a red neon Tio Pepe sign. Ahead, there was nothing but a steady trail of people who seemed uninvolved in the protest. That was the direction she'd first headed, and the one she kept going in.

She didn't know where she was going or what she would do when she got there, but right now she couldn't sit in that car with him and know he'd spied on her. An image of Parker Gaines—his smooth lies, the voice recorders he'd used to capture their conversations, the humiliating meeting with her father—flashed into her mind, and she thrust it out again with a growl.

The cobblestone walk sloped upward, toward an archway in the medieval buildings. She kept walking, hoping it was similar to the place Alejandro had taken her years ago. If so, there were cafés, restaurants, places she could disappear and sit for a while, until she felt like returning to Alejandro's villa.

And she would have to return, wouldn't she? All her things were there. Even her purse, with her driver's license and credit cards. *Oh, for the love of God.* She ground to a stop while the foot traffic flowed around her. She had no money. She didn't even have a cell phone.

A hand settled on her shoulder and she whirled around, a little scream escaping as she stumbled backward.

Alejandro caught her to his big warm body, squeezed her before setting her away carefully. He loomed over her, so handsome and imposing in his tuxedo. She thought he looked concerned, but she must have imagined it because the next second his face was set in a harsh mask.

"Madre de Dios," he swore, shrugging out of his tuxedo jacket and placing it around her shoulders. "What were you thinking, taking off like that? I thought you were ill!"

"I'm not," she said. "Or I won't be if you leave me alone."

The jacket was still warm from his body. His scent surrounded her. She wanted to shrug the garment off, but she realized she was shivering. From adrenaline or cold she wasn't certain, but she clasped the jacket around her and held it tight like a shield.

"We will return to the car," he said.

Rebecca shook her head like a recalcitrant child, but she didn't care. "No, I'm not getting back in that car with you. You *spied* on me, Alejandro. I hate you for that."

One eyebrow quirked. "More than you hate me for taking Layton International away?"

She ground her teeth together and turned her head. "It's different."

"Tell me why."

Rebecca pulled in a deep breath, tilted her head up to look at him. His expression didn't mock her like she'd expected. He looked truly curious, as if he didn't understand why she would be so upset about him prying into her life. Why would he? Why would anyone?

"It's not the first time it's happened," she said, unwilling to share more than that. "I don't like it. It makes me feel... violated."

"It was an investigation, not a robbery. This is common enough in business, yes?"

Too common in *her* life. He couldn't understand. No one could. "It doesn't make it right."

"It was business."

"Everything with you is business. But I don't believe it, Alejandro. You brought me here because you wanted to hurt me, pay me back for what you think I did to you. Well, you've succeeded. Are you happy now? Can I go back to New York and forget I ever met you?"

"You would give up so easily? Leave Layton International?"

"Do I have a choice?" Why was she pushing him? This wasn't part of her plan. She needed to stay, needed to keep involved in the day-to-day operations, or she would lose the insider track to all that happened with her company and would never get it back.

"Perhaps you do," he said softly.

She sucked in a shaky breath. "What's that supposed to mean?"

"Come back to the car," he said. "We will go home."

Home? How could one word evoke so many feelings? But

it was his home, not hers. She had no home. Her apartment was a place to sleep and store clothes. The family home had been sold when her father had died. Her mother had moved back to Paris. The only place that felt like home was La Belle Amelie, and that was because of her connection to the place, the fact she'd been born there when her mother's water had broken a month early.

Where was home now? She honestly didn't know.

"I'm not getting back into that car right now," she said. "If you try to force me, I'll scream."

Alejandro's expression went from sober to amused. "Did you not see the protest, *amor*? The *policía* are very busy at the moment. I could drag you back by your hair, like a good caveman should, and no one would notice."

She turned her head toward the archway, ignoring him. Why was it when he gave her that little half-smile she melted into a puddle? Though she was angry with him, his humor threatened her heart in a way nothing else could. She had to focus on something else, something other than the man in front of her. "Is that like the place you took me?"

"*Sí*. It is the same—the Plaza Mayor. There are several entryways."

She loved the way his voice caressed the sound: Plaza MAY-orrr. She remembered a beautiful square, similar to Venice's Piazza San Marco, though much more colorful and uniquely Spanish. There were restaurants, *tapas* bars, and shops beneath the portico that ran around the perimeter.

It was also the place where Alejandro had first kissed her. Sitting at a sidewalk café, sipping sherry, he'd leaned over and kissed her sweetly on the lips that first time. It had been everything she could do to accept the chaste kiss, not to curl her hand around his neck and demand more of him. He'd set her on fire with one touch of his lips.

In truth, she should want to run screaming from a memory

such as that. But the prospect of getting back into the car with him right now was even more frightening. "I want to go see it."

He studied her for a long moment. Was he remembering the kiss too? Or, more likely, wondering if she planned to bolt again. "Explain to me what happened in the car."

She fiddled with the edge of his jacket. "It was a panic attack, Alejandro. Nothing more. I'm not sick. But if I get back in the car right now I might be. I just need space."

Space without him in it—without him invading her senses and making her question everything she thought and said.

He rubbed a hand over his face as if he were about to make a choice he didn't want. "*Sí*, fine—we will go."

"We?" She wanted to be alone, not shadowed by this hulking shell of a man, not reminded at every turn that he'd betrayed her trust more than once.

His mouth twisted. "You think I will allow you to go alone? No, this is not possible. What if you were to have another attack?"

"I won't."

"How can you be sure?"

"Because it rarely happens. I can't even remember the last time." A lie. She remembered very well the last time she'd had an attack so bad she couldn't breathe: the moment she'd climbed into the taxi after leaving his suite five years ago. She had mild attacks from time to time, but it took exceptionally powerful emotion to make it difficult for her to breathe. "I just want some time to myself, out in the open, without you stalking after me."

"This is not an option, Rebecca. We go together, or we return to the car."

She pinched the bridge of her nose. "Fine." She sighed. "Let's go."

He tipped his head toward the jacket. "If you will permit me to get my phone? I must tell Garcia where to pick us up."

Rebecca nodded, and he parted the material. His fingers

brushed the swell of her breast as he reached into an inner pocket and she shivered involuntarily.

When he'd finished, they walked in silence to the archway and passed beneath, emerging into a huge square lined on all four sides by a portico. Painted figures adorned the portion of the facade stretching between two clock towers. All around the square, tables and chairs were set out from the restaurants. At this hour patrons were eating dinner. It always struck her as odd that Spaniards ate so late. At least there were *tapas* for people like her.

"Which café did we drink sherry at?" she asked.

Alejandro pointed to one of the arched openings leading into and out of the square. "There, near the Arco de Cuchilleros. Do you want to go?"

"No." She almost said yes, but decided it would be too much to revisit the memory in the exact spot. She was already tempting fate simply by walking through this *plaza* with him. She moved out into the square and turned slowly around, gazing at the buildings and balconies. Anything to take her mind off the man before her.

Alejandro stood casually, his hands in his pockets. His white shirt stood out against the darkened square. He was still wearing his bow tie, which she found immensely sexy for some reason.

"There are two hundred and thirty-seven balconies and nine entrances," he said.

"It's very beautiful." *He* was beautiful, damn him. Beautiful and lethal.

He shrugged. "The Inquisition once put heretics to death here."

"Yes, well, we have nothing like it in New York. Central Park, maybe—but that's a park and not a town square."

Violin music began to drift from the portico. It was soft, haunting. A street musician playing for tips, most likely.

Rebecca closed her eyes, blocking out Alejandro, and swayed to the music. So pretty, so peaceful. Inevitably she remembered making love with him beneath a moon-drenched sky while violin music drifted from the radio in the rooftop suite. Did he remember it too?

"I know what you are thinking," he said, his voice soft and sensual—and closer than she'd expected.

Her eyes popped open to find him hovering over her. She stopped swaying and gazed up at him. How could any one man be so attractive? He was like a fallen angel with his dark hair and mesmerizing stare.

"No, you don't," she replied, her heart thrumming in her breast.

He slipped an arm around her, hauled her closer. "Oh, *sí,* I do. I am thinking of it too."

Her brain sent the signal to back away, but too late. His other hand grasped one of hers, placed it on the hard muscle of his bicep. Another pull and she was flush against his body.

Breast to belly to hip. His arousal came as a surprise and her breath broke on a gasp.

"Yes, I want you," he said.

"But you hate me."

His easy grin had the power to light the dark corners of her soul. He was so much like the old Alejandro in that moment that it made her ache.

"And you hate me. This does not stop our bodies from desiring one another, *sí?*"

She realized he was swaying them in time to the music, guiding her in a slow and sensual dance. And she suddenly didn't want to be anywhere else. Her body recognized his, answered with the sweet ache of desire. Her feminine core grew damp and her breasts felt heavy, needy.

She closed her eyes, gave in to the temptation to press her cheek to his chest. His heart beat loud and strong beneath her touch. Quick, but not racing like hers. Whatever this was, he was affected too.

They moved slowly, silently. His hand slid down her back, over her buttock, and she shivered, her senses on full alert. She was like a finely tuned instrument awaiting the right hands. His hands. It had been so, so long.

"Madre de Dios," he said a moment later, pulling away from her. He didn't stop the dance, didn't break the contact, but he put space between them.

"What's wrong?"

He gave her a meaningful look. "Nothing…if we were alone." His fingers skimmed her jaw, her throat, the material at her collarbone. Sparks of sensation trailed in their wake, shivered across her heated skin.

She was frozen as he tilted her chin up, dipped his head toward hers. His lips brushed across her mouth so lightly, like the touch of a butterfly wing. She wanted more, parted her lips in anticipation, but he pulled back. His breath whispered over her moistened lips.

"I want to strip you slowly, kiss every centimeter of your skin and make love to you for the rest of the night."

Rebecca gulped. Oh, God, she wanted it too.

But she couldn't. She couldn't lose her head over this man. Not ever again. And after tonight—the pain in his eyes as he had held his sobbing mother, the raw wound of losing his baby, her realization that his desperate need for control stemmed from tragedy and heartbreak, and that her own family had contributed to his losses—how could she keep her heart hardened to him?

Desperately, she seized on the bad things she knew: he'd stolen her company, he'd had her watched, he thought the worst of her. He didn't respect her as a person, didn't think she was good or honorable. He was acting on pure male instinct, animal attraction. He wanted her body, nothing more.

"I—I can't," she said, casting her eyes down, away from

his burning gaze. She slipped out of his embrace and spun blindly toward the portico. They could never go back to where they'd been before. It had been foolish of her to come here, to dance with him, to remember another, more innocent time. To open herself to the vortex of emotion that he caused inside her.

Life did not go backward. It ground forward relentlessly. If she'd endured the car, they might still be in the Puerta del Sol, but at least her heart would be intact.

Her fault. She'd allowed this to happen. What had she been thinking when she'd wanted to come here?

She was almost under the portico when he caught her, spun her around and pulled her into the shaded area of an archway. His body was hard against her, his hands framing her face. His warmth seared her skin. Her back hit a column and she realized he'd trapped her between him and the stone.

"You're mine, Rebecca," he said vehemently. "For as long and as often as I want you. I have bought and paid for you many times over. You will not deny me."

Then his mouth crushed down on hers. It was the wildest, hottest, most devastating kiss she'd ever experienced. And when it was over, when he let her go and stepped back, breathing hard in an effort to regain his icy control, all she wanted was to wrap her arms around him and make him do it again.

They didn't speak on the ride back to the villa. Rebecca huddled against the door and watched the night lights of Madrid slide by. She had no idea what Alejandro was thinking. And she didn't want to ask. *That* kiss. God in heaven, she'd have done anything he asked at that moment. Thankfully, he hadn't repeated it. He liked toying with her. She realized that now. He liked to get her teetering on the edge of her emotions before he flung her off the cliff and onto the rocks below. He had no intention of seducing her, only of proving to her again and again how vulnerable she was to him.

It was after midnight when they entered the darkened interior of the house. There was no sign of Señora Flores, or any of the other servants. A light burned softly in the Great Room, spilling out into the hall, but nothing stirred.

Though every instinct told her to flee, Rebecca paused in the foyer. Alejandro stood with hands in pockets, watching her closely.

Say goodnight—get away. "Thanks for…um…understanding when I didn't want to get back into the car right away."

"You said it wasn't the first time someone had you investigated. Who did so before?"

Rebecca removed his jacket from her shoulders, folded it over her arm and held it out. "You better take this now, before I forget."

He tossed the jacket aside, caught her wrist and held her still when she would have fled. "Rebecca?"

Irrational tears clogged her throat. "Goodnight, Alejandro." She didn't want to talk about this, most especially not with him. To share her humiliation with the one man who'd ever meant anything to her? Who'd rejected her so brutally? Impossible.

His grip tightened as she tried to pull away, preventing her from moving even a fraction. It was like playing tug-of-war with a tank.

"You don't have to tell me," he said. "It's not at all necessary for what happens now."

She stopped trying to extract herself from his grip and stared up at him, her pulse beginning to hum erratically. "I want to go to bed."

His smile was predatory. "*Sí*, as do I."

"Alone, Alejandro."

His arms encircled her, his fingers stroking down the

exposed skin of her back, trailing fire in their wake. "This is not possible, *querida*. I have told you what I intend."

Her palms came up to press against his crisp shirtfront. "You can't mean it. You can't want to make me do this."

One brow lifted. "*Make* you do this?" His fingers skimmed her spine, up and down, up and down, eliciting shivers along her nerve endings. "I think I will not need to make you do anything. You want me, Rebecca. You have wanted me since the moment you arrived."

Damn him for throwing the truth in her face. Yes, she wanted him, but she also wanted chocolate after every meal. She didn't indulge because it was bad for her. *He* was bad for her.

"No," she said firmly. "You are mistaken."

"I'm not," he replied, his lips a fraction above hers now. "And it doesn't matter anyway. You are mine."

This time when he slanted his mouth over hers she held herself firm, refused to break. He ran his tongue along the seam of her lips, slid his hands down to grasp her buttocks and pull her into the cradle of his hips.

And, oh, my, he was blessedly, hugely, gloriously hard. *For her.*

But she would not break. Her sanity depended on it, on holding part of herself separate from him. She knew more about him now than she ever had before, and that knowledge threatened to enslave her heart in spite of everything he'd done to her.

Why did she feel this pull, this intense storm of emotion, over *this* man? Why not David, her long-suffering and incredibly patient boyfriend, who'd finally left her over a year ago because she couldn't ever love him the way he'd wanted her to?

It wasn't *fair*.

"*Dios,*" Alejandro said against her tightly closed mouth.

"You are determined to fight me." His lips moved along her jawline, down her throat. Before she realized what he was doing, he slid his fingers beneath the shoulders of her dress and jerked it forward, down her arms, trapping her with her naked breasts exposed to his gaze.

"Alejandro, let me go—someone could see!"

"I thought you could not be wearing a bra beneath this," he said, almost to himself, his eyes hot as they moved over her. "I have wondered about it for hours."

The way he looked at her made her breath shorten. *Like he wanted to worship her.* She could almost forget she was standing in his foyer, bare to the waist, her nipples peaking beneath his scorching gaze.

"What else aren't you wearing, Rebecca?" he asked, his voice a sensual purr.

She couldn't speak as his hand slipped into the back of her dress. Soon enough he would know. His groan told her even before his hand settled on her bare bottom that he'd realized she wasn't wearing any panties.

"The material is too clingy," she babbled. "There would've been a line…"

"This comes off," he said. "Now."

"No, Alejandro—wait. What if someone sees me?" she said as he started to tug the material down.

"They won't." He skimmed the expensive jersey from her body until she stood in nothing but high heels and a puddle of fabric. Then he took a step back, perusing her thoroughly. "You are exquisite, Rebecca. I have waited too long for this."

Her brain kicked into gear as her skin prickled from the cool air of the foyer. The man had servants, and he'd undressed her in a public area of his house. And she just stood there like a museum exhibit while he ogled her! Anyone could come along at any minute.

She reached for her dress, but Alejandro was there first, scooping her into his arms.

"No," he growled. "I want you in my bed. You will not need any clothing for many hours yet."

CHAPTER EIGHT

A DIFFERENT kind of panic was starting to grip her by the throat as Alejandro carried her into his bedroom and kicked the door shut. She was naked in his arms, he'd brought her to his room, yet she still believed he somehow meant to shame her beyond her wildest imagination.

This was a ruse, she was certain of it, and she began to kick her legs back and forth, trying to force him to put her down.

"Be still," he said. A moment later she was on the bed and he was hovering over her, his fully clothed body pressing down on top of her. "Tell me," he said, his lips on her jaw, her throat, her collarbone. "Tell me you do not want this, Rebecca, that your body does not ache for mine…"

His mouth fastened over one aching nipple and she arched her back, cried out. He gave her absolutely no time to adjust to the feelings assailing her body. His fingers slid between her thighs, parted her, found the sensitive heart of her.

"Alejandro," she gasped.

"Tell me you don't want me," he said, his breath hot against her body as he moved to her other nipple, sucked it between his lips.

She shuddered, her body alive with more sensation than she'd felt in a very long time. Even the other night in the pool she hadn't quivered like this, hadn't thought she would die with every slick pulse of his fingers against her, inside her.

She was on the edge so quickly it shocked her, ready to tumble into an orgasm just from the feel of his tongue on her nipples and his fingers inside her. But he stopped, said heated words in Spanish, while he sat up and ripped at the studs on his shirt. She looked up at him, her heart tumbling over in her chest, breaking for the millionth time because of him.

But she couldn't stop herself from reaching for him, from raising herself until she could touch his jaw, press her hand to his skin, her fingertips sliding down to his lips, over them.

Those beautiful lips had given her more pleasure than she could ever have imagined. He'd been the first man to make love to her with his mouth. She'd never told him that.

Now he'd gone completely still as she touched him, his gaze hot and intense as he watched her.

She slipped a finger into his mouth, over the front of his teeth, across the tip of his tongue. When she would have retreated, he gripped her hand gently, sucked her finger in and out, his heated stare never leaving hers.

"Alejandro," she whispered, her blood pounding in her veins, her heart ready to burst from so much feeling. She hated him, she loved him, she hated him. Her heart ached and ached and ached until she thought she might die from it. What was this feeling really? Why couldn't she work it out?

"Sí, mi amor?" He kissed her palm, her wrist, the tip of each finger.

She'd said his name because of the maelstrom inside her, but he responded as if he expected a question.

She could think of only one. "Did—?" She swallowed the knot clogging her throat. She had to ask, had to know. "Did you love her?"

Until that moment when she'd learned he was engaged, or

supposedly engaged, her life had seemed so right with him. She wanted to understand how it had gone wrong. Why.

He lowered her hand to his chest, pressed it to the hot skin he'd exposed when he tore his shirt open. She could feel his heart, fast and strong, and her fingers trembled.

His eyes, hot as they were, somehow managed to be flat when he answered. "I have never loved any woman. I never will."

She didn't feel any relief to know he hadn't loved his wife. And though she'd known he hadn't loved *her*, it still hurt to hear it so starkly stated. "Poor Alejandro," she said softly. "You must get so lonely."

The shock on his face might have been comical if she hadn't known what he'd suffered. He would never admit it, but there had to be times when he would be relieved to share the burden of so much sorrow. To have someone understand. To love him.

"No more talking, Rebecca," he said. "No more questions." He pushed the shirt from his shoulders, stripped off his trousers and kicked them free, then stretched out over her. "Just feel—feel what you do to me, what we do to each other. *This* is what's real."

His mouth captured hers, and this time she opened to him, tangling her tongue with his as he stoked the fires in her body once more. Part of her was terrified of what was happening, and part of her wanted it more than her next breath. She knew she should go—should shove him away and leave this bed before she lost more than her pride.

But she couldn't do it. Her body sang beneath his, wanted his, seemed made especially for his. She wrapped her legs around him, opened herself to him. He rose above her on his palms, gazed down at her with a look she couldn't decipher.

She felt him pushing at her entrance, sliding forward just enough to make her pant, then withdrawing again.

"Alejandro, please. *Please, I need you.*"

He growled low in his throat, then surged forward in one

long, gliding stroke. She cried out with pleasure and shock as he filled her. He was bigger than she remembered, and his possession was intense.

He didn't move, though she could feel the pulse beat of him deep inside her.

He looked uncertain. "Did I hurt you?"

"No, no—it's okay. It's been a long time."

His eyes glazed as she moved her hips, learned how to accommodate him again.

Finally he spoke, seemed to drag his thoughts from somewhere. "A long time? You have not—?"

She rolled her head back and forth on the pillow.

He looked surprised. Fierce and possessive. "You should have told me. I would have been gentler."

"Ohhh," she gasped, as he pulled out and glided back in. "Noooo, you wouldn't have believed me."

"Rebecca," he groaned, dropping his head. She didn't know if he meant to say more, if it was agreement or denial, but he flexed his hips and she no longer cared.

He moved slowly at first, each thrust measured and sure. Trying not to hurt her. But he was so careful she wanted to scream. She ran her hands feverishly down his body, over his biceps, the scar on his side.

"Alejandro, I won't break. Make love to me. *Please.*"

His mouth crushed down on hers, their tongues mating while their bodies merged harder and faster. He lost whatever control he might have had, his movements quickening until he was pounding into her with all the passion of a man long denied. She kept a tight control on herself, thought she might hold out forever, but he slipped his hand between them, stroked her where their bodies joined.

Her orgasm didn't just slam into her; it stole her breath and brought her up off the bed as she arched into him, sobbing her pleasure. A second later Alejandro lost the hold he'd had on himself, his hips pumping into her harder as he groaned her name brokenly.

He collapsed on top of her, breathing hard. She ran her palms down his back, over his buttocks, sighed heavily. It was a glorious, earth-shattering mistake to make love with this man. She knew it, but she tried to hold the regret and pain at bay as long as possible.

He'd won, hadn't he? He'd stolen her company, dragged her halfway around the world and stripped her bare—both literally and figuratively. She had nothing left, not even her dignity. Soon he would get up from the bed, look at her with disdain and order her out of his sight.

When he lifted himself on his elbows he was still breathing hard. The look in his eyes was not what she'd expected, and it ripped her heart in two. Confusion, anger and passion collided in that one smoldering gaze.

He kissed her softly, almost sweetly. Her heart, she feared, was lost forever.

Moonlight drifted through the windows and arced across the bed, waking him. Alejandro lifted his head, momentarily disoriented. Why hadn't he closed the blinds before lying down?

It came back to him quickly, crashing into his mind in a series of images and sensations.

Dios. He turned his head slightly, gazed at the woman sleeping beside him. She'd curled up in a ball at the edge of the bed, as far away from him as she could get. Perversely, it angered him. She'd tried to get away from him when they were awake and had not succeeded. In sleep she won the battle.

He slipped the covers off and padded to the window naked. His body was satiated in a way it had not been in months. In spite of his feelings for his self-absorbed ex-wife, he'd stayed faithful to their marriage vows until the day the divorce had become final. In the months since, he'd slaked his thirst with many women. Anonymous, uncaring sex had been a balm to his ravaged soul.

Or so he'd thought.

Until tonight, when he'd lost himself in the gorgeous and willing body of the woman he hated most in this world. For those few hours he'd forgotten.

But he did hate her. He pressed a knuckle to his temple.

It was all according to plan. Bed her, make her care, ruin her. He owed it to Anya. He would do this for Anya. Anya, who should have lived. Who should have been his and Rebecca's child.

He clenched his fist, pressed it to the glass. He had done nothing wrong. He had not miscalculated. Never mind that she'd been untouched for so long, or that she'd seemed to see into his soul in the limo tonight. She was shallow, calculating. She slept with him now to try and gain an advantage. And how did he know he was really her first lover in a long time? She could be lying, faking. But if it were a ruse wouldn't she have told him earlier, tried to elicit his sympathy?

He took a deep breath, let it out. Sometimes his mind raced between so many possibilities that he couldn't keep up.

"Alejandro?"

He turned and went to the bed. Moonlight limned her features, her very messy golden-blonde hair, her kiss-swollen lips. Desire lifted its slumberous head inside him.

"I am here," he replied.

She clutched the sheet to her. The scent of sex clung to her. To him.

A new thought prickled at the back of his mind. Something he should have thought of long before now. *Sweet God in heaven, he'd forgotten to use protection.*

"I should return to my room," she said, unaware of the stark fear snaking down his spine.

"No," he said coldly.

She seemed to shrink in on herself.

"Are you protected?" he demanded.

Her head quirked to one side. "Wha—? Oh, yes. Yes," she said more firmly. "I'm on the pill. I thought you knew that."

"How would I know this?" he asked, stupefied that she would think so.

Her chin lifted. "I thought your private investigators would have told you."

"It was not that kind of investigation," he defended. Still, relief threatened to liquefy his knees. *Madre de Dios, gracias.* This was the first time he'd ever forgotten to take precautions. It was not at all like him, but he chalked it up to the mental exhaustion of dealing with so much angst and drama tonight.

On the heels of relief came a surge of lust so strong he felt it from his scalp to his toes. A second later he peeled the sheet from her grasp and laid her back on the mattress, his hands skimming up the insides of her thighs, pushing them apart.

"I've been dying to taste you," he said.

He loved her soft cries and moans, the slick sweet taste of her, the way she arched off the bed and screamed his name when she came. He didn't let her stop at one climax; he spread her wide and laved her with his tongue until she was panting and moaning again, until a fine sheen of moisture glistened on her skin, until his name was a hoarse cry on her lips.

And then he was inside her, losing himself as he thrust hard, again and again, unable this time to be gentle. He had no control, no finesse with this woman. He came in a hot hard rush, groaning and gasping like he'd run a marathon, then rolled to the side and gathered her against him.

They lay on top of the sheets. Her body twitched every now and then—aftereffects of the powerful orgasms he'd given her. It made him feel possessive, proprietary. His fingers trailed up and down her arm almost absently.

"Who had you watched, Rebecca?"

She jerked in his arms. She must have been nearly asleep, but now she grew rigid, her body vibrating with a different kind of tension.

"It doesn't matter."

"I want to know."

She pushed away from him, rose up on one elbow beside him. Her nipple brushed his arm and he felt the jolt to his groin.

"I don't want to talk about it. You don't really care. All you'll do is be smug." She traced a finger around one of his nipples, followed with her tongue. A ploy to distract him.

But her words pricked him. He didn't care that she'd been hurt by someone, it was true, but he wanted to know anyway. It fed his need for control.

"Was it a lover?" He spat the word.

She lifted her head. "No."

"A rival?"

She laughed bitterly. "Yes—you."

Who else would possibly want to investigate her? Not a lover or a rival. Unless she was lying. It had to be a business rival. Who else? Why else?

A tendril of intuition niggled at him. Who could hurt her so badly by spying on her? "Family?"

She stiffened, and he knew he had his answer.

He twined his fingers in her hair, drew her down to him. Kissed her deeply. "You can tell me, *querida*. I want to know."

She sighed, her shoulders slumping before she fell back on the bed and put an arm over her face. "Fine," she said. "What's it matter anymore?"

But she didn't say anything for so long he thought she must have fallen asleep. He bent to kiss the soft skin of her breast. She let out a little sigh and he rolled her nipple between his lips, suckled it into a sharp peak.

"I can't think when you do that," she said, on a soft susurration of breath.

He propped himself beside her, fingers stroking little circles on her skin. "Was it your father?" Truly, he couldn't see anyone *but* Jackson Layton hiring a private investigator to follow his own daughter around. And he didn't entirely disagree with it. He could imagine doing the same thing if Anya had lived. Anything to keep her safe.

"Yes." One word, nothing more.

"You will not tell me more?"

She shook her head, her eyes tightly closed, and he felt the sting of disappointment. She'd told him nothing at all. Once she would have told him anything he asked.

That time was gone forever. It was just as well. He did not need to feel pity for her.

The next morning Alejandro's business necessitated his return to Dubai. There was a break in the standoff over permits, but he needed to be there personally in order to ensure a smooth resolution to the problem.

The last thing Rebecca had expected was to be ordered to accompany him. In truth, she hadn't known what to expect after their night together.

Alejandro knew. "You are my mistress," he said, when she asked why he wanted her to go.

She'd nearly choked on the word. "Mistress? Until a few days ago, I was the president of a major international hotel chain."

His smile wasn't at all friendly. "*Sí*, until a few days ago." He tossed something into his briefcase, then speared her with a silver glare. "And not so major, *no?*"

"Does this mean you're considering selling me some of the stock?" she asked, knowing it was the wrong thing to say, yet angry enough to hurl at him what he'd said to her in the pool anyway.

Her amazing lover of the night before was gone; in his place was the ruthless businessman who'd stolen her company. In the stark light of day she had to wonder how she'd managed to forget all the hurt and betrayal long enough to fall into bed with him.

His expression was so cold she had to suppress a shiver. "It means you are my mistress. Nothing more."

When they landed in Dubai that afternoon, a black Mercedes limousine met them at the airport and ferried them to the resort Alejandro had recently bought on the Jumeirah coast. It wasn't as grand as some of the other hotels, but his plans to expand it would make it one of the top destinations in Dubai. If the permit situation was resolved.

A man in a tuxedo hurried forward to greet them when the car doors opened, snapping his fingers at a bellhop who leaped into action to collect their luggage from the trunk.

"Señor Ramirez," the man said as Alejandro stepped from the car. "We are so pleased you are back with us again. Your suite is prepared. Shall I make reservations for dinner, or will you be dining in?"

"In the suite, I think, Ali."

"Very well, sir."

The suite was truly a gorgeous place. Situated on the top floor, its view of the Persian Gulf was spectacular. Rebecca went onto the balcony, gazed out at the sparkling blue water, the ship traffic and the glorious sail-like structure of the Burj Al Arab hotel silhouetted against the hazy sky in the distance.

Palm trees swayed in a gentle breeze near the beach. Directly below her was the pool. Guests dotted the chairs while waiters moved back and forth between them. Behind her, she could hear Alejandro on the phone. He didn't sound happy.

It was strange, almost exhilarating in some respects, to be here and not be the one working. Not that she *wasn't* working. She had her phone and her laptop, and she was still—so far—

in charge of day-to-day operations at Layton International. But not to be the person fielding frantic phone calls about permits and construction issues—it was bliss. She could see, off to the left, the area where construction cranes sat silent. No trucks moved, no workers—nothing happened in the fenced-off site. Every day was money. He could afford a lot, she was sure, but at a certain point he would need to cut his losses.

She went back inside. A bank of windows ran along the front of the suite. Automatic blinds closed with the press of a button, though they were open now, to allow the afternoon light inside. A plush living area contained a couch and chairs, a bar and an entertainment system with a flat-screen television. There was a dining area near one window. The bedroom had a giant king-size bed piled high with pillows, but it was the sunken tub in the bathroom that caught her eye. The floors were marble, and marble columns surrounded the tub on four sides, making it look like a Roman bath. A peek inside told her there were jets. Heavenly. Maybe she could have a nice long bath while Alejandro went to meet with government officials.

He came into the bedroom as she was leaving the master bathroom. He wore a dark polo shirt and khakis, and his hair was mussed. He'd been raking his hands through his hair again—no doubt the result of his phone call. Perversely, she wanted to smooth it back into place.

"It meets with your approval?" he asked, nodding toward the bathroom.

"It's nice."

"Merely nice?" He seemed a little irritated.

"No, it's very nice."

His face darkened. "It is spectacular—far better than many of your own hotels. Which I will rectify, I assure you."

She stamped down on the hot anger rising to the surface. He was baiting her. He'd had bad or frustrating news and he was taking it out on her. Amazingly, the realization only made her calmer. "Of course, Alejandro."

He stalked closer. "You are making fun of me?"

She shook her head. "No."

He reached out, trailed tanned fingers down the vee of her blouse, toyed with the top button. "Take this off."

Her breath shortened. The anger she'd stamped down deep was beginning to bubble again. "I'd rather not," she forced out.

"And I say you have no choice."

She drew herself up and leveled him with her best glare. "There is always a choice, Alejandro. I choose *not* to be ordered around like a paid-by-the-hour hooker. If you need to sell a hotel or two, or dismantle Layton International and scatter it to the wind to punish me, then indulge yourself. You can't control every single minute of my life with your threats. Save them for the big stuff."

His face was dark, unreadable. And then one corner of his mouth lifted in a grin. It was like sunshine breaking through after a violent storm—and completely *not* what she'd expected. "You amuse me at the oddest moments, *bella*."

He caught her around the waist, tugged her against his body. "My meeting has been moved to tomorrow morning, and I find I have many long, empty hours to fill." He dipped his head, touched his lips to her nose, her cheeks. "Help me fill them, yes? I want to spend the afternoon in bed with you…"

"I'm not your employee when we're alone like this," she insisted, still angry—though her blood was humming for an altogether different reason now. "You can't order me around in the bedroom like it's a boardroom."

He kissed her hard, broke away. "You would not obey me in the boardroom either," he whispered. "Not without a fight."

"If you would ask instead of order," she said, gasping as his fingers slipped inside her shirt, her bra. He softly pinched her nipple into an aching point. "You get more flies with honey, Alejandro…"

"Please, Rebecca," he said with a predatory gleam. "*Let* me taste you."

Rebecca didn't see Alejandro very often over the next couple of days. He was up at daybreak, meeting with government officials, touring the construction site, trying to get to the bottom of the permit situation. But when she did see him—

Oh, my—it took her breath away to think about it. The man was insatiable, and he worshipped her body with a thoroughness bordering on obsession. She found it impossible to say no.

Rebecca sighed and stretched her naked—and very satisfied—body. She was still sprawled on top of the covers, where he'd left her when he went into the shower. He'd tried to get her to join him, but she couldn't move. She'd been surprised to see him back so early, but he'd burst into the suite and announced he'd had a breakthrough. A few phone calls later—half of them conducted in English—she partially understood what was going on. Alejandro had a corporate spy, who'd been working with another company to hold up the construction process.

He'd been almost gleeful. She liked seeing him happy. He used to be happy all the time when she'd known him before. Marriage and tragedy had changed that.

"What are you thinking about so intently, *amor*?"

Rebecca looked up to find him watching her. He stood beside the bed, the towel slung low on his hips, every delicious inch of his rock-hard chest displayed for her delight. Her heart jumped, the way it always did when he was near. She hadn't heard him come back.

"Will you tell me what happened to Anya?" She wasn't sure where the question came from, but she realized she'd been thinking of his little girl a lot lately. About how such a tragic loss had changed him from the man she'd once known.

There were still glimpses of that man, but he was buried under the weight of tragedy, under the hardened husk of what he'd become.

She wanted to know, wanted to understand.

His eyes closed, snapped open again. She thought he would walk away. His jaw hardened.

"She was born with a congenital heart defect," he said. "It should not have been fatal, had it been diagnosed when she was an infant. But she was one of the rare ones."

Rebecca sat up, reached for him. He'd been in a good mood, and she'd managed to destroy it. He moved away before she could touch him. She clasped her arms around her knees. "I'm so very sorry. For both you and your wife."

The pain in his features was evident—the drawn mouth, the tight jaw, the flared nostrils. "Three-year-olds should not have heart attacks."

"No." Her throat ached. She wanted to get up and wrap her arms around him, press his head to her breast and hold him.

Alejandro's skin had paled beneath his tan. She'd have never believed it had she not been staring right at him.

"I shouldn't have asked. I'm sorry."

"No, she is gone now, and people always ask. I must become accustomed to it."

How did you ever get accustomed to such a thing? A vile, sorrowful, evil thing that was the death of a child?

She didn't know what else to say. She simply wanted to hold him.

But he started to shrug into his clothes, his back to her. "I have work to do. If you wish to go shopping or sightseeing, please inform Ali. He will arrange for anything you need."

Without a backward glance, he was gone.

Alejandro was restless, keyed-up, jumpy as a caged bull before a fight. He drummed his fingers against the center armrest in the limo, thought about the woman he'd left in his bed. Why had he told her about Anya? She'd surprised him with the question, but he'd surprised himself even more by answering it.

He did not want to share such things with her. Anya was none of her business. He should have choked on the words before spilling his guts to a woman like her.

A woman like what?

A woman who melted beneath him, who made him crazy with her little sighs and moans, who fought him when he pushed and who insisted on being treated with respect and dignity in spite of his plans for her?

He was going soft. Just because his body craved hers, just because he showed no signs of tiring of her—indeed, each time he made love to her he seemed to only want her more— it was no reason to lose sight of what he meant to do. He had to ruin her. He'd planned it for so long, lived for it through the darkest days. He couldn't cease now.

It was time to start knocking the foundation out from beneath her, if only to prove he could do it. He would start tonight.

CHAPTER NINE

A TEAM of waiters arrived to serve dinner in their suite. Rebecca had been surprised when Alejandro returned in time for the meal. Usually she ate alone, working on her computer since it was still only mid-afternoon in the States. She accomplished a lot in the hours Alejandro was away, even if part of her anticipated his return with growing excitement as the day waned.

She'd worked through the afternoon, but she'd been pre-occupied with their conversation earlier. She couldn't imagine losing a child so cruelly. It was senseless, surreal. The grief he must have experienced was unimaginable.

And yet he'd endured it. He'd changed because of it, but she understood why now. Looking at him across the table, her heart filled to bursting with everything she was feeling toward him, she knew without a doubt that she was falling for him again.

Or perhaps she had already fallen, but she wasn't quite prepared to admit it to herself just yet. No, far better to look at him in his cream silk shirt, with his dark hair and skin such a startlingly beautiful contrast, and imagine that she had time to prevent the disaster she was hurtling herself into. He'd barely spoken since returning. She wondered what dinner would be like—how she could draw him out if he didn't speak.

Maybe she should apologize for asking him about his daughter. But she wasn't sorry he'd told her. It helped her understand. Helped her forgive him just a tiny bit for how he'd treated her since he'd ordered her to Madrid.

The sommelier uncorked a bottle of wine and poured a taste for Alejandro's approval. After the wine was decanted and the food served, all but one of the waiters left. The man stationed himself near the buffet where they'd set the dishes, and prepared to serve as needed.

"I have decided to move Layton International's offices to Madrid," Alejandro announced.

Rebecca nearly dropped her fork. The spicy rice and eggplant dish she'd just taken a bite of turned to paste in her mouth.

"You seem surprised," he said, his dark gaze giving nothing away.

She reached for her wineglass, took a fortifying sip. Her heart was beginning to flutter at breakneck speed. "I am. You haven't told me your plans for my company, and now this. What about my employees? There are over one hundred people in the New York office."

He shrugged. "Upper management will be offered jobs in Madrid. Others will be given generous severance packages and assistance in finding new employment."

"Is this because I asked you about Anya?"

His eyes flashed. "No. It's business."

She set her fork down and leaned back against her chair, no longer hungry. "Oh, really? Somehow I don't think so. I know you're angry with me, but it's unfair to take it out on my people."

He tapped long fingers on the tablecloth as he studied her. She would not think about what those fingers did to her each night. She kept her gaze firmly on his face.

"I do what's best for Ramirez Enterprises. It has nothing to do with you. They are *my* people now, not yours."

She didn't believe he did this for the good of Ramirez. Clearly he was punishing her—especially when he pointed out that she wasn't responsible for her employees any longer.

"I owe them, Alejandro. My family owes them. I can't sit by and do nothing."

"You do not have a choice. When you chose to pledge your stock as collateral for those loans, you took the risk that someone else would gain control of your company. You no longer have a say in what happens at Layton International."

That was the bitter truth, wasn't it? No matter how much it hurt, how much she disagreed, she had no legal ground to stand on.

"What about me?" she asked. "Am I fired now?"

He took a sip of wine, watched her over the top of his glass. Several seconds went by before he spoke. "Not yet."

Her relief was palpable. And yet it was suddenly too much. Everything—the way he'd manipulated her into doing what he wanted, his threats, the juxtaposition of cold businessman with white-hot lover—she couldn't take it a moment longer.

"I'm not sure I can continue this way," she said softly. Her appetite was gone, so she set her napkin over the plate.

Alejandro glanced at the waiter. A signal must have passed between them, because the man bowed and disappeared.

"Continue how, Rebecca?"

"I want to know what your plans are for me. I'm tired of wondering."

The sudden heat in his eyes wasn't what she expected. "My plans involve the bed, the shower, and maybe even this table."

A current of awareness snapped between them. But she couldn't simply fold like a house of cards. "I was talking about business, Alejandro."

"So was I. This is the business of being my mistress."

He looked amused rather than annoyed. It irritated her. Did

she have the strength to walk away from his seduction? From him? She pushed her chair back and stood. Alejandro's gaze sharpened. He looked like a great cat scenting prey.

"Where do you think you're going?" he asked.

"To the front desk to ask for my own room." She went to retrieve her purse and briefcase, her pulse tripping along in her ears like a racing piston.

"Yes, run away, Rebecca. It is what you do when things are difficult, *sí*? Better to run than face the problem."

She whirled around and marched back to the table. Her entire body shook as she stared him down. "You aren't a god, Alejandro. You can sit in your ivory tower and order people around, you can destroy companies and lives, but nothing will bring back your child. *Nothing.*"

It was so obvious, and yet he was blind to it. He was consumed by rage and grief, and reacting every day to those forces in his life because he hadn't yet learned how to deal with them.

He shot to his feet. But she didn't stop. She couldn't. She tumbled on. "You accuse *me* of running away? What in the hell do you think *you're* doing? You've been running since the minute she died and you don't even know it!"

"Get out," he growled.

Rebecca refused to cry. "Yes, that's exactly what I thought you'd say. Far better to order me away than to face what you're feeling. But you won't always be able to run, Alejandro. One of these days it's going to catch up with you."

"You need to leave," he said gravely. "Now, before I—"

"Before you what? Make me regret the day I was born?" She drew herself up, laughed. But inside she was dying. "For once you're too late."

The trip back to Madrid was accomplished in silence. Alejandro watched Rebecca from beneath lowered eyelids.

She concentrated on her laptop screen, never looking at him. She'd spent last night in her own room, several floors away from his. He hadn't gone after her, much as he'd wanted to.

Madre de Dios, the things she'd said to him. He'd spent the rest of the night tossing and turning, thinking about it. Was she right? Was he running from Anya's death?

He shoved the thought aside angrily. What did she know? She'd never experienced such a loss, never sat in a waiting room alone and waited for news, never spent hours trying to locate a woman who was attending fashion week in Milan and couldn't be bothered to turn on her cell phone.

She had no idea what she was talking about!

He needed to end this. He didn't need her chipping away at him like she could break the ice surrounding his heart. It was painful, uncomfortable. She made him feel like he was on the brink of losing control, like the balls he kept spinning in the air could crash down on his head any minute.

When they landed in Madrid, he needed to tell her she was done. Tell her in the airport so she could catch a flight out. Say goodbye forever.

He leaned back against the headrest, closed his eyes. No, he had to be more deliberate about it. He'd planned it for so long. He couldn't tell her in a public place like an airport.

And he couldn't tell her now because he didn't want to deal with the dramatics for the rest of the flight. He would tell her tonight. *Sí*, this was best.

He would seduce her one final time, use her luscious body for his pleasure. And then he would ruin her life the way she'd ruined his.

After they landed, Alejandro sent Rebecca back to the villa while he went into the office. He had things to do, and he needed time to think. He'd waited so long for this day. He wanted to do it right—wanted to enjoy the full measure of her despair.

Except he looked on it with dread more than anticipation. Why? Perhaps it was the prospect of drama, of her tears and pleading. He'd once thought that would be gratifying, but now he realized he just wanted the whole mess over cleanly and quickly.

But maybe he was wrong to move so fast. It had only been a couple of weeks since he'd taken over Layton International. He needed to enjoy the full measure of his triumph, needed to watch her squirm for a while in his employ. She would think she had a chance of regaining her company and he would know it wasn't possible. In the meantime, he would enjoy her in his bed.

Yes, a much better plan. In fact, he would take her to the opera at the Teatro Real tonight. He would make nice and be solicitous. She would fall into his arms willingly when they returned home.

Señora Flores was in the entry when he came through the door a couple of hours later. She frowned at him, spun on her heel and marched away. Rebecca's suitcases were stacked off to one side.

"You're back."

His head snapped up, his gaze landing on Rebecca. She stood in the door to the office. She was dressed in a tailored gray pantsuit and carried her briefcase.

"You are going somewhere?" He'd warned her what he would do if she left. Did she think to manipulate him by threatening to walk out?

"Yes." Her chin tilted up as he moved toward her. She looked as if she wanted to flee, but she stood her ground. He took in her defiant stare, her red eyes, the puffiness—

"You have been crying, *querida*? What has happened?" Had something happened to her mother, perhaps? He would order his plane to be made ready—would take her anywhere she needed to go.

He moved to embrace her, but she shrank away so quickly he thought she might fall. "No," she gasped. "Don't touch me."

His arms fell to his sides. *Madre de Dios*. Why was his chest suddenly tight?

"Tell me," he commanded, retreating to ground he understood. He would force her to do his bidding, to tell him what was wrong.

In answer, her hand snaked out, connected with his cheek. He didn't even flinch. Their gazes clashed and held. A disconnected part of him idly wondered how this would end. But the warrior in him knew what was in store. He could see the violence shaking her in its grip.

A moment later she rushed at him, her hands balling into fists. He grabbed her wrists, held her away from him as she struggled.

"Rebecca, for God's sake—tell me what is wrong." As if he didn't have an idea.

She sucked in a breath, wrenched herself from his grasp with a strength that surprised him. Spinning away, she wrapped her arms around her body.

She faced him again, glaring. "You *own* the bank, Alejandro. You've owned it for over a year. The *only* bank that would loan my father money!" She laughed. The sound broke off into a sob. "I thought it was a mistake at first—that you'd bought it recently, along with the promissory note for Layton International's loans. But *you* financed the loan. And *you* sold the Thailand resorts to us. They belonged to you, to one of your subsidiaries. You set everything up. When you said you make your own luck, I thought you'd watched us and waited. But you *made* everything happen!"

He shrugged, tried to look casual. Unfeeling. "*Sí*, it is as you say."

She took a step forward, her fists clenching so hard her knuckles were white. "He *died* in Thailand. Touring the resorts *you* sold him in order to ruin us. My God, you *are* a bastard. How I could've thought—" She swiped at her eyes, shook her head.

"How did you learn this?" Her face was pale, her expression almost fragile. Oddly, it bothered him.

"It's too ironic, really. Roger Cahill e-mailed me the documents. He dug them up while looking for dirt on you. Funny, huh?"

"You have been in touch with Cahill?" It shouldn't surprise him, but it did. Cahill had been the financial power behind the company fighting him over the Dubai property. No doubt she'd been in close contact with him the entire time—though she'd been in no position to learn anything truly useful to report back. Strangely, the thought she would even want to stung him.

"I asked him what happened five years ago," Rebecca said, sniffling. "Perhaps you should have done the same."

"I know what happened," he snapped. How many times did he have to remember it?

"Not really," she replied, her chin thrusting out as she drew herself up. "My father killed your deal—so, yes, the Laytons tried to ruin you. I think he must have been angry because you hurt me, but I don't know that for sure. I suppose you can blame me if you want, but you need to blame yourself as well. If you hadn't had a fiancée—or whatever you want to call her—none of this would have happened."

Blame himself? What the hell was she talking about? It was *her* fault. He took a step forward—to do what, he wasn't sure.

The doorbell rang and he stopped, shook his head. Señora Flores's footsteps pattered down the hall.

"That'll be my taxi," Rebecca said. "I recommend John Barnes as the new CEO."

Surprise rooted him to the spot. This was not the way it was supposed to happen. *He* was the one in control—the one who determined when and how everything happened. She could not walk out on him again! "You are running away? What about your company?"

"What should I do? Stay and wait for you to fire me?" She shook her head. "Layton International's not mine anymore, is it? You've made sure of that. Now it's time I got on with my life."

When she shouldered past him he gripped her arm, a feeling he didn't understand seizing him in a choke hold. "This isn't over."

She shuddered in revulsion. Her gaze settled on his hand, lifted to meet his stare. "Yes, it is. Goodbye, Alejandro."

She picked his hand off her arm. The touch of her skin seared him. He had a primeval urge to grab her, haul her to the bedroom and lock her inside until she smiled at him again. Until she made love to him like he was the only man in the world.

But he didn't say anything as she turned and walked to the door. What was there to say? He'd won, hadn't he? He had Layton International. Rebecca had nothing. It was what he'd dreamed of for five years.

He didn't know how long he stood there, but when he finally looked up long shadows had crept across the tiles. It was over. Rebecca was gone.

New York in summer was predictably sweltering. Rebecca made it back to her air-conditioned apartment building before she wilted, and headed for the elevator. She didn't want to think about what she'd just bought at the drugstore, but there was no getting around it.

Fishing in her purse for her keys, she stopped in front of her door. Twenty minutes later, she stared at the test stick. Pink. She knew what that meant. How had it happened? She hadn't missed her pills at all. She'd had some breakthrough bleeding, and the doctor had said her body had grown too accustomed to the pill she was on. So he'd given her a different one about a month before she'd gone to Madrid.

She dropped the stick, her heart pounding with so many emotions. Joy, yes. Pain too. In the mirror, her face was pale. Drawn. She had dark circles beneath her eyes, and she'd lost weight. Her chest rose and fell quickly as she worked to control her rioting emotions. She would not panic.

Her baby needed her to be healthy—not this pale, sickly creature who couldn't eat or sleep properly. Her hand fluttered to her abdomen, pressed against her womb. She was pregnant. With Alejandro's baby. Already she loved this child fiercely. She wanted to run and pick up the phone, call Alejandro, tell him how wonderful and terrifying the news was. But she couldn't.

He didn't care about her. He never had. Everything with him was about control.

Rebecca shoved a trembling hand through her hair. *Oh, God.* What was she going to do? She was alone, and now she had another life to think about. How could she work and take care of her baby at the same time? Because she *had* to work. She hadn't paid herself a salary since her father had died, and her savings were nearly gone. Who would take care of them both if she didn't?

Her mother? God, no. Alejandro? She crushed down a hysterical laugh at the thought.

It had been four weeks since she'd left Madrid. Four excruciating weeks. She'd actually believed he might come after her. That he might apologize for all he'd done and beg her forgiveness. What a delusional fantasy!

She could still see his face so clearly when she'd confronted him. He hadn't denied a thing. He'd looked cold and disconnected, like he didn't care that he'd turned her world upside down.

She was still staggered by the depth of his betrayal. He

hadn't just watched Layton International from afar. He'd found her father's weakness, enticed him into the loans and the Thailand properties, and kept twisting the knife even after her father died. Twisted until he'd won the battle. She'd been devastated when Roger had sent her the proof, and she'd reacted in the only way she knew how.

Leaving her company hadn't been easy, but it had been necessary. She could no longer allow Alejandro to control her life. For her own health and sanity she'd had to go.

She'd been angry and bitter. She'd even thought for a brief time that she had hated him. But her father had made his own choices in life. Alejandro might have manipulated the situation, but Jackson Layton had not been a puppet. He had wanted the Thailand property in spite of the best advice against the acquisition, and he'd single-mindedly gone after it.

His death had been unexpected, but she couldn't truly lay it at Alejandro's door. If it hadn't been Thailand, it would have been something else. Her father had been a bit of a daredevil—skydiving, rock climbing, bungee jumping, swimming with sharks—and it was a wonder he'd lived as long as he had.

Rebecca splayed a hand over her abdomen possessively. There was no denying how she felt about Alejandro any longer. When had she fallen again? When he'd found her with the photo album? When he'd looked at her with such naked need in the suite at the Villa de Musica?

Or had she never stopped loving him?

Not that it mattered how or why. She loved him. Love wasn't something you turned on and off like a faucet, however much she might wish it so. She was in love with the man who'd ruined her. And she was carrying his child!

The nights were the worst. So lonely. She hated sleeping alone in her bed so much she'd finally dragged a blanket to the couch and now slept there. She missed Alejandro's big warm body, his intense lovemaking, the rare smile that changed his features and bound her heart.

He obviously did not feel the same. He hadn't called, hadn't followed her, hadn't even written an e-mail. He wasn't tortured by sleepless nights and memories. The only thing she'd received from Spain was a severance check from Ramirez Enterprises.

She was on her own now. She'd returned to New York to pack up her apartment, and then she was on her way to London to take a job with the Cahill Group.

But with a baby on the way? They'd made a baby together. It was a miracle, an amazing, beautiful miracle. *Oh, Alejandro, I want you to know. I want you to love us.*

Rebecca swallowed. She didn't know how to be a mother. She'd always been busy with her career. She had friends with babies, but she didn't understand how they knew what to do. Her own mother would certainly be no help. The woman didn't have a maternal bone in her body. What if Rebecca didn't either? How could she possibly put a baby through the sort of neglectful existence she'd endured?

She drew in a shaky breath. It rattled out again and ended in a sob.

She had to tell Alejandro. For a moment she considered pretending the baby was someone else's. But she couldn't do it.

Not after Anya. He'd loved her, and he would love this child too, no matter how much he hated the baby's mother. But how to tell him and make sure he didn't try to take their baby away from her? Because she had to acknowledge it was a very real possibility. He hated her so much he would have no qualms about ripping her baby away and making her suffer.

And she would *never* allow that. This baby was hers, and she loved it more than she'd ever loved anything in her life.

She wasn't telling him today. Probably not even tomorrow. She'd tell him when she'd figured out how to deal with him and let him know in no uncertain terms that he wasn't taking their baby away from her.

The next few days were a blur. Between doctors' appointments and preparing for the move to London, Rebecca didn't have much time to herself. The movers would be here tomorrow, and she would fly the day after that. It was all so fast, but that was how she wanted it.

She'd stopped at the bookstore on her way home and picked up two books about pregnancy and one on mothering. Who knew they had such things? But thank the Lord they did, because she would need all the help she could get. She still hadn't figured out how to integrate this new life inside her with the one she knew—long days at the office, endless meetings and business trips—but there had to be something in these books that would help.

She thought of the evenings when she'd used to sit at the window and wait for her daddy to come home. Her mother, if she noticed, would say, "Your *père* is working, *ma belle*. He will be home when he can. Now, go play and stop your moping."

How could she do her job and make sure her child didn't feel as lonely as she had? Because she couldn't imagine this baby sitting at a window and waiting for her to come home. She would not let it happen. Her baby would know it was loved, cherished. Somehow she would make everything work. She had to.

Bernadette, the daytime door attendant to her building, rocked back and forth on the balls of her feet and smiled as Rebecca approached. Her blue uniform was always crisp, her smile always ready. Rebecca would miss the woman's cheery greetings.

"Miss Layton, good to see you. How's the move going, hmm?"

"It's a pain, but I think I'll survive," she answered. Her days had been so busy that she was behind on many of the things she'd wanted to accomplish, but she made a mental note to give Bernadette an extra-large tip and a gift before she left.

Bernadette leaned forward, her eyes flashing. Rebecca grinned. What manner of hunk had the woman seen now? Bernadette was always talking about the good-looking men in the building, or the ones who'd strolled by during the day. It was one of the highlights of her job.

"Supreme eye candy alert," she said. "A foreign type. Got out of that limo there and entered the building not more than five minutes ago. Bet he's on his way to that beauty queen's digs."

They had a former Miss Something or Other in the building, which seemed to fascinate Bernadette no end. Any time a good-looking guy went inside, she was convinced he was headed for the woman's apartment. She was probably right.

"How do you know he's foreign?" A little twinge of sadness hit her as she pictured Alejandro's incredible smile. Whoever this guy was, he couldn't compare, she was certain. No man could.

"Oh, honey, I can spot 'em a mile away. But he was on the phone, and it wasn't English he was talking. Smelled like money too, let me tell you." She wagged her head back and forth. "Mmm-mmm, I'd sell my soul to the devil himself for one night in the sack with that guy. He'd never know what hit him."

Rebecca laughed and left Bernadette to her daydreams about Miss Whatever's potential suitor. Taking one of the books out of her bag, she flipped through it while she waited for the elevator.

So much to know about babies. Unconsciously, her hand drifted over her abdomen. She smiled when she realized what she was doing.

"We have a lot to learn, you and I," she said to her baby. It didn't matter if the baby couldn't understand her yet; it comforted her to talk to her child. *Her child.* Those words still gave her a little thrill. And, funny enough, she no longer felt so alone in the world, knowing she had a life growing inside her. They would be okay. Somehow they would be okay.

She hummed a little as she walked down the hallway toward her apartment. A familiar scent seemed to linger in the air as she reached her door, and a trickle of alarm buzzed between her shoulder blades. It wasn't a heavy cologne smell, but a scent that came from expensive clothes and a certain brand of soap. Her heart pounded into her throat as she shoved the key in the lock and pushed the door open. She closed it behind her, slid the chains in place, and let out a shaky sigh.

What was the matter with her? Alejandro was *not* here. He couldn't be here. He had no reason to be. He didn't know about her pregnancy. And though he'd had her followed once before, he had no reason to do so now. He was finished with her. No investigator was lurking outside her building, sending reports to her gorgeous Spanish lover.

To the father of her child.

Rebecca shivered. Her senses were heightened due to the hormones rocketing through her system. The man visiting the beauty queen was simply cut from the same mold as Alejandro—rich, handsome, and possessed of impeccable taste. He eschewed cologne and used imported soap. So what?

She set her bag of books on the coffee table and went into the kitchen to get a glass of cool water. There were boxes everywhere. She surveyed the open loft, the amount of work yet to be done. Despair crushed down on her.

Though the Cahill Group was paying for her relocation, it didn't help her in sorting through her things before the movers arrived. She had to keep busy or she'd go crazy.

The doorbell buzzed and she sighed. Janine from down the hall had mentioned a get-together in her apartment this afternoon, but Rebecca didn't feel like going. Still, it was just like Janine to try and talk her into it—especially when she was leaving in two days.

"Just a minute," she called when the bell buzzed again. When she reached the door, she checked the peephole out of habit.

The man standing in the hall was definitely not Janine.

Her breath shortened, her heart plummeting to her toes before shooting through the roof. How could she deal with him? Why was he here? What would she tell him about the baby?

Tears flooded her eyes as she folded her hands over her belly protectively. No, she wasn't ready. If she didn't say anything, maybe he'd go away. What in hell was Alejandro doing in New York? Maybe he'd had her watched after all? Maybe he knew everything? Cold fear dripped down her spine.

"I know you're in there, Rebecca. Open the door."

CHAPTER TEN

REBECCA closed her eyes. That voice, the crisp Spanish inflections. The sound sent a wave of longing through her. And fury. How dare he show up *now* and demand she open the door to him? Where had he been a month ago? He should have been here, apologizing, begging her forgiveness. *Right.*

"Rebecca—open up or I'll kick it in."

She'd like to see that. The door was steel. And yet he was making enough noise that any second doors would start popping open up and down the hall. Worse, she believed he really would try to batter her door down if she didn't answer. She yanked it open, but didn't undo the chain.

Alejandro stared down his nose at her. His arrogant, rotten, deceptive nose.

And he looked every bit as delicious as he had over a month ago. He wore Armani, of course. The tailored gray suit made him look elegant and commanding. Every inch the captain of industry. He was so amazingly beautiful to her eyes. Any second her heart would crack wide open, and she'd be spilling her secrets to him.

His gaze raked over her. "You are unwell?"

Did she look that bad? Her doctor had said she was healthy, if a little underweight. Alejandro had probably moved on to some elegant, gorgeous woman who simpered and put up with his moods. She felt dowdy and unattractive just thinking about it. And heartbroken.

"I'm fine. What do you want?"

"I wish to talk with you."

"Start talking."

He nodded at the door. "Can I come in?"

"No."

He pushed a hand through his hair, blew out his breath in annoyance. "It would be easier to let me in, would it not? Or do you prefer your neighbors hear what I have to say?"

She had no idea what he would say but, no, she didn't want her neighbors to hear it. She shoved the door closed and slid the chain back. Besides, her stomach chose that moment to roil. All she wanted was to sit down and get this over with. She jerked the door open and turned her back on him, going over to sit on the couch and fold her legs beneath her. Hostility was her only armor. She prayed he would not see beneath it.

He came inside, his gray gaze coolly assessing his surroundings. He seemed unsurprised she was moving. Of course. He probably knew everything about her job with the Cahill Group. No doubt he saw it as a betrayal that she would work for Roger, but what else was she supposed to do?

"You look unwell," he said again as he strode into the living room. His hands were thrust in his pockets. He was so tall, so imposing. And he was standing in her apartment, his presence reminding her of all they'd done together. Her heart throbbed with anger and hurt.

She shook her head. "It's nothing. What do you want?"

"You didn't cash your severance check."

Rebecca blinked. "You came all the way to New York to say that?"

"No. I came to meet with Layton International's board."

She swallowed a wave of tears. He was here for business, not for her. It seemed so strange to hear something about her company from him. A board meeting that she wasn't a part of. Hadn't known about.

"Just tell me what you want and get out," she said wearily. Her brain had gone numb. She couldn't deal with him—couldn't begin to imagine telling him about the baby she carried. When she got to London and got settled in she'd give him the news. He'd be angry, but this was her body and her pregnancy and she'd do things her way.

He reached into his jacket and pulled out an envelope. When he tossed it onto the coffee table, she eyed it warily. "If that's another severance check, you can keep it. I don't want your money."

Perhaps if Roger hadn't hired her she would have been forced to cash it. But now that he had, she had no intention of taking a dime from Alejandro. He'd once called her greedy. Let him wonder why she wouldn't accept money from him.

"It's not."

Rebecca heaved a sigh and leaned forward to grasp the envelope. Maybe if she opened it he would leave. Sadness washed over her, but she pushed it away and ripped the packet open to stare at the contents.

Dashing a hand over her cheeks to wipe away her tears, she tried to sound flippant. "I should refuse, but I won't." She clutched the deed, more touched than she wanted to be. She wasn't going to take his money, but she would take this. One day she would give it to their child.

"No, La Belle Amelie is yours."

"I'll pay you for it. Just give me time to put together the financing."

"No."

Rebecca sucked back tears, forced a laugh. She didn't know how to respond, so she resorted to flippancy. "Honestly, Alejandro, the sex *was* pretty good, but I doubt it was worth quite this much."

His mouth opened, then closed as his gaze fixed on something lying on the table. His head turned, as if he was trying to read—

She scrambled for the bag of books she'd knocked over reaching for the envelope and shoved them back inside. Before she could stash the bag beneath the table Alejandro had ripped it from her grasp.

His expression was a mixture of horror and rage as he yanked a book out and stared at the title. Eyes hot with emotion pinned her like a bug. "What is the meaning of this?"

She considered for about half a second telling him the books were for a friend. But she couldn't do it. This baby was his too, and, God help her, she still loved him. She wanted him to know—wanted him to be happy about it. And she was terrified at the same time. Terrified he would be angry, that he wouldn't believe her, that he might try to take the baby away.

No. She would never allow that. Never. He'd already taken the one thing that had meant the most to her. He would not do so ever again.

"Surprise," she said softly, her throat as dry as noon in the Sahara.

Soul-deep fear riveted Alejandro in place. Pregnant? She was *pregnant*? He shook his head to clear it. No, this could not be.

"How did it happen?" he said, his voice very cold and controlled.

Her expression crumpled a little, then hardened as if she were determined not to show any weakness in front of him. "The usual way, I imagine. We certainly had enough sex, don't you think?"

"You are telling me you're pregnant." It was a statement, not a question.

"Yes, Alejandro. I'm pregnant."

"How do you know the baby is mine?" She'd left him five weeks ago. Plenty of time to dupe some other man into believing she cared for him. Roger Cahill, perhaps? The man was only about twenty years her senior—still perfectly capable of being her lover.

Her face whitened. She shielded her abdomen with a hand. "How could you ask such a thing? Of course it's yours! The doctor estimates seven weeks."

Alejandro dropped the book on the table and raked a hand through his hair. *Dios.* If this baby were really his, how could he go through it again? How could he live each day wondering if it would be the day his baby would die?

Anya. Her little body turning blue, the trip to the emergency room, the frantic efforts to revive her. *Dios, no.* Her eyes haunted him to this day. He would never survive it a second time.

Hurricane-force emotion whirled inside him. Which was the easier to digest? Rebecca sleeping with another man so soon after she'd left him—which would require the doctor to be wrong about the dates—or the knowledge her baby was his and might very well be vulnerable to the genetic defect that had taken Anya's life?

Solving the baby's parentage would be easy enough to do, though he very much feared it was unnecessary; she was telling the truth. He went over to where she sat on the couch, her expression one of hurt and misery. She tilted her head back to look up at him.

He would not be moved by what he saw in her face. "You said you were taking the pill. Did you lie? Did you do this on purpose, thinking it would gain you Layton International?"

She shot up from her sitting position, but he was too quick for her. Grabbing her wrist, he prevented the slap she tried to deliver. Her blue eyes reflected hurt and surprise. Awareness shot through him at the contact of skin on skin, though it was only his hand on her wrist. He wondered if she felt it too. What would she do if he lowered his head and kissed her?

He wanted to. The compulsion shocked him.

She jerked free and moved out of his reach. "You can be so vicious, Alejandro. Why do you always need to think the worst of people? Sometimes things just happen."

He rolled a shoulder irritably. "I'm a wealthy man, *querida*. It wouldn't be the first time a woman thought to gain advantage by claiming I'd fathered her child."

Her jaw went slack.

"I have had one child, Rebecca, in spite of what you might think. Fatherhood is not a responsibility I take lightly."

"I'm glad to hear it, for our baby's sake. But I am—*was*—on birth control. It was a new prescription and it obviously didn't do the job it was supposed to do."

He took his mobile phone from his pocket and called the airport, giving instructions to ready his jet for takeoff.

"What are you doing?" Her voice sounded strained.

He ignored her.

"Alejandro?" The sound was sharper this time.

He pocketed the phone and prepared to do battle. "We are returning to Madrid tonight."

She folded her arms beneath her breasts. He ignored the arrow of heat knifing into his groin. Had her breasts gotten fuller? *Sí*. As if she wasn't beautiful enough already. Need washed over him. To strip her slowly, to lick his way from nipple to nipple, to drop lower and taste her before thrusting hard into her—he very much wanted to do all these things, and often. For a month he'd thought of almost nothing else.

"Have a nice flight," she said. "Glad you could stop by."

He bared his teeth in a smile he knew she couldn't mistake for a friendly overture. "I do not use the royal we, *amor*. You are coming with me."

She paled. "No. You aren't taking this baby away from me, Alejandro. I'll fight you with everything I have."

"And what would that be, Rebecca?" He stalked closer, satisfied when she backed away. He was too furious to play games with her. "I have more money and more resources at my disposal than you could ever hope to muster in a year of phone calls to all your former contacts. You *will* accompany me."

Her throat worked. "Why are you doing this? I have a job in London. I have a life—"

"Your life is with me now. You will pack a suitcase, *inmediatamente*, and come with me."

"This is America, Alejandro. You can't kidnap me and force me onto a plane. We have laws against that."

He laughed. Cute of her to try and dissuade him with the threat of the American authorities. And completely useless. He would do anything—no matter how ruthless, no matter how underhanded—to win this battle with her.

"Nevertheless, you belong to me. You will cooperate, or I will make sure you never see this child again after it is born. I will use any means necessary to win. Do not mistake me."

Her breathing grew faster as she battled some emotion. Tears, no doubt. But he would not be swayed if she lost control. He knew he was being harsh, but icy sharp fear had him in its grip. He would protect this child at all costs. He would never, ever allow Anya's fate to strike again. This baby would be tested within an inch of its life. So would he. And so would Rebecca. He would leave nothing to chance.

"Why do you have to be so cruel?" It was little more than a whisper.

The barb pricked him. But he had no use for misguided attempts to imbue him with guilt. "Life is cruel. Better to face the bull head-on, *sí*?"

She sank back onto the couch, her breathing irregular. The

hairs on his arms prickled. *Dios*, she'd had trouble breathing once before—when he'd upset her.

He dropped to his knees in front of her, gripped her shoulders. "Breathe, Rebecca. All will be well. Come with me and I will take care of you both. I promise you."

She dropped forward until her forehead was touching his, pulled in deep breaths. He cupped her jaw in both hands, smoothed his thumbs over her cheeks. "Shh, *mi querida*, don't fight. Think of something happy, yes?"

"Easy…for you…to…say—"

"Kittens," he said. "Kittens are happy. Or puppies. *Sí*, think of these things. I will buy you a puppy. Or a kitten. Or both. Just be calm," he said softly, caressing her slowly, rhythmically. His heart battered his ribs as he worked to soothe her. *Because of the baby—it is only because of the baby…*

"You will *not*…take…my baby. Not—"

"No." What else could he say? It was imperative she be healthy for their child.

"Your…word."

Cold conviction dripped down his spine. He knew what he had to do, though it filled him with dread. "You don't need my word, *amor*. You will have my name."

How could she possibly marry him?

A week later Rebecca was still wondering how she'd agreed to get on that plane and return to Madrid. She'd been terrified when he had threatened to take her baby away by fair means or foul. After what he'd done to get Layton International, she did not doubt he was capable of anything.

But even that hadn't been quite enough to tip her over the edge. No, it was the way he had touched her so sweetly, the way he had soothed her with his beautiful, sexy voice. His fingers on her skin, sending shards of sensation through her. Giving her his strength, helping her get through the panic.

She'd loved him so much in those moments that she'd have agreed to move to Mars if he'd asked her to. Worse, she had been able to deceive herself—briefly—that he loved her in return simply by the sweetness of his touch.

It certainly *had* been self-deception, because he hadn't touched her since. She did not know if he ever would.

Rebecca pressed her temples against the headache flaring to life. She'd quit her new job, followed him to Spain like a lovesick puppy, and he'd barely spoken to her. He was probably still laughing at how easy it had been to convince her.

But it *was* the best decision for their child. She knew it down deep. Alejandro would be a good father, a fierce, protective father. His child would never be an afterthought in his life. She was comforted by that knowledge.

For herself, however, a lifetime of heartbreak lay ahead. He'd gone to extraordinary lengths to get her company, yet the real punishment would be in living with him and loving him when he did not return the feeling.

How would she endure it?

She would simply have to. But she could never allow him to know the power he had over her. While she could trust him with their child, she could never trust him with her heart. It would be a lonely existence, but she would survive it. And once their child came along she would have someone to love, someone who would love her unconditionally.

Unexpectedly, Alejandro arrived home that afternoon to collect her for her doctor's appointment. She protested that she could go alone, but he would hear none of it. Because of what had happened to Anya, she didn't fight him over it. He had a need to be there—a need to be involved and understand everything that happened with her pregnancy. He wanted to protect the baby. If it helped him feel somehow in control of the future, she wouldn't stop him.

The appointment was routine. Alejandro was sensible enough about her wish not to have him there for the pelvic exam, but he returned immediately after. They both had blood taken for the genetic testing Alejandro insisted on having, though the baby couldn't be tested for heart defects until much later. The doctor assured them that if they both were fine, the baby most likely would be too.

Later, when they were in the car on the way back to the villa, Alejandro said, "We need to set a date for the wedding. Have you called your mother?"

Rebecca turned to look at him. She'd been watching the people on the sidewalks as they passed by. She didn't know what to say to him anymore. He was like a stranger to her. When they talked it was about the baby or the wedding, nothing more. And that was only sporadic.

"She hasn't returned my call yet."

He looked surprised. Rebecca shrugged. She was accustomed to her mother's shallowness by now. "She's probably shopping. Or skiing."

Disapproval hardened his expression. "Do you want to wait so she can be here for the ceremony?"

She picked at a thread on her cardigan. "It's not necessary."

Silence. Then, "My sister wants to meet you."

"I'd like to meet her, too." He'd always spoken with affection for his sister. She was nervous about the prospect of meeting Valencia, but curious as well.

"She is arriving soon for a short visit. We can be married while she's here, if that is agreeable."

Rebecca fiddled with her bracelet as she digested this information. He hadn't mentioned his family at all since she'd returned. "Does she know about the baby?"

"*Sí*, I have told her."

Which meant his sister knew why they were marrying so quickly. "And your parents?"

"They will know soon enough."

She wasn't sure what to think about why he hadn't yet told his parents. "What will they think about you marrying me?"

He gave her a significant look. "They won't care. They are far more interested in their own lives than in mine or my sister's."

She heard the bitterness in his voice. She hadn't forgotten what he'd said to her in the car the night they'd returned from his parents' party. And after her brief time in Juan and Carmen Ramirez's company she knew it was probably the truth. They reminded her of her own mother: selfish and self-absorbed.

"They will not be at the wedding?"

His laugh was sudden and sharp. "You don't want them there, believe me. They would somehow manage to turn it into a personal drama where they occupied center stage."

"You had a lavish wedding before," she said. "I believe even the King and Queen attended." She'd looked up the photos on the Internet. Alejandro had been spectacular, his bride gorgeous—but neither of them had smiled much.

"There is no time for this kind of wedding," he said coolly. "You would be big with our baby by the time we married. We will have a quick civil ceremony and be done, *sí*?"

She pushed her hurt down deep. It wasn't that she wanted a huge wedding—she just wanted this to be about something more than a marriage of convenience to him. She also wanted to understand why he'd married his first wife, since he claimed not to have loved her.

Something he'd told her tickled her mind. "You said the night of the anniversary party that your father wanted to chase me away five years ago. If he cared who you married then, why not now?"

Alejandro sighed. "It wasn't you specifically, Rebecca. He wanted me to marry my brother's fiancée."

"I don't understand."

"My father arranged a marriage for my brother. It was a

matter of family honor to him. When Roberto died, it fell to me to keep the agreement."

"Your brother died before you met me. If you were to marry her in his place, then you were already engaged." She felt tears pricking her eyes. Stupid hormones. This was old news.

Alejandro's brows slashed down. "No. I had no intention of marrying her, in spite of my father."

"But you did anyway. Did our sheets even get cold before she moved in?"

"You left *me*, Rebecca."

She lifted her chin and met him dead in the eye. "It took me almost a year to see someone else. Yet you were married and expecting a baby by then."

It was hard to admit the truth, but why hide it any longer? He acted like he was the one who was wronged. What about her? She *wanted* him to know how difficult it had been for her.

His look was intense, curious. "You did not take a new lover? Why should I believe this?"

"You can believe what you want, Alejandro." She lowered her eyes, toyed with the hula girl charm on her bracelet. "I've never been the sort of woman who falls into bed with whomever strikes my fancy. Not that there's anything wrong with it, but I always had to be careful."

Alejandro stared at the top of her head. All this talk about marriage was closing a vise around his neck. He had every intention of marrying her, of binding her to him so he had legal rights to his child, but the thought of it always made anger burn low in his gut. He would marry her, but he didn't have to enjoy the prospect. Sometimes he wondered if he'd been expertly maneuvered into it. He tried not to consider that possibility very often.

But what was this about being careful who she'd slept with? Her attention was firmly fixed on the gold bracelet she wore. He wanted to reach out, clasp her arm and make her look at him. But he did not.

"What do you mean, *querida*?"

"My father. Layton International," she said, never looking up.

He thought back to how upset she'd gotten when he told her he'd had her investigated. Suddenly it made sense. And he thought that if Jackson Layton were here now, he'd throttle him. "Did your father have you watched all the time?"

Her head snapped up. Tears glinted in her eyes. Something tightened in his chest. He reached up to rub absently at the spot, realized what he was doing and dropped his hand again.

"He might have. I don't really know any longer." She laid her head back against the seat, closed her eyes. He found himself thinking how fragile she looked. She'd been almost a shadow of herself when he'd seen her in New York last week. Since returning to Spain he'd put Señora Flores to work feeding her. She had more color in her cheeks, and she was starting to fill out a little bit. Soon she would be big with his child. The thought made him possessive.

"Why would he do this to you?"

She took a deep breath, let it out again. "Because I was a girl, Alejandro. He wanted a son to leave the business to." She looked at him. "He thought I would be weak, that I would lose my head over a man—because that's what women do, naturally."

"Not you," he said, and meant it. One of the things he'd always been impressed with was her sense of the hotel business. They'd spent hours talking about every aspect of the business when he had still been new to it. And after he'd taken her company he'd watched her in the boardroom, reviewed her management of Layton International, and realized who'd really steered the company into a freefall. The only weak Layton had been her father.

"He had cause to think so," she said quietly.

"Because of me?"

"No, someone else."

Something very like jealousy sliced into him. "You were in love?" She'd told him she loved *him*. He'd believed it until she'd betrayed him. But to think she'd loved someone else, really loved him? He had an urge to slam his fist into something.

"It was a couple of years before I met you, the summer I was twenty," she said. "Parker Gaines was very sophisticated, very suave. He was a con man—though I didn't know it, of course."

She bowed her head, spoke to her lap. "My father wanted to test me. Or so he said. He hired Parker to 'breach my defenses' as he put it. I was young enough and—" she laughed bitterly, brokenly "—lonely enough to believe Parker's lies. He seduced me, claimed to love me and stole money from me. Worse, he got the combination to the safe in my office. He stole documents, checks, plans for future developments. Father was livid."

Alejandro seethed with fury. *Dios*, had her father been insane? He did not doubt for a moment that she spoke the truth. She was too devastated, her fingers trembling as she talked, her voice breaking on the name *Parker Gaines*.

"Why would your father do this?"

She shrugged, as if it didn't mean anything, but he knew that was far from true. "He wanted to teach me to be ruthless. He called me to his office after I'd discovered the extent of Parker's theft. And Parker was there, drinking Scotch and smiling like he'd won the lottery. He'd recorded our conversations, played back some of the juicier ones for my father while I stood there and tried to defend myself." She sucked in a shaky breath. "God, it was humiliating. But I learned my lesson. I was very careful who I let into my life after that."

She was supposed to be a spoiled heiress, not this ravaged woman pouring out her private pain to him. Alejandro didn't know he'd reached for her until he gripped her hand in his, felt the small bones and cool skin. "I'm sorry that happened to you, *querida*."

Though he would never say so to her, he was also glad her father was dead. It saved him the trouble of killing the man himself.

She didn't say anything, just nodded, her head turned toward the window. When her shoulders shook silently, he squeezed her hand. Nothing more. Though it went against every instinct he had not to drag her into his arms and hold her.

Why had she told him those things? Rebecca splashed cool water on her face and looked at her red-rimmed eyes in the mirror. Was she insane? He'd been horrified, like any rational person would be, but he'd viewed it more as a curiosity outside his sphere than as something that touched him personally. He'd been kind, but no more.

What had she expected? That he would enfold her in his arms and kiss her tears away? Take her to his bed and make love to her? If she'd hoped for a connection with him she'd sorely miscalculated. She had to be careful, had to keep her feelings hidden. She would not give him that kind of power to hurt her ever again.

When they had arrived back at the villa he'd wasted no time getting away from her. He'd gone into his office and shut the door. She didn't blame him. It was a pitiful story, but not truly tragic in the way losing a child was.

Rebecca pressed her hand to her stomach, her heart fluttering at the thought. "You will be well, little one. I know it," she said. "Your daddy is big and strong, and you will be strong just like him."

For the rest of the evening she didn't see Alejandro. He was still in his office, door closed, when she returned from the kitchen and Señora Flores's wonderful *paella*. She could hear him barking out orders to someone on the other end of the telephone line.

Though she didn't remember going to bed, it was dark when she opened her eyes. She was floating, falling, her back landing on cushiony softness. Something covered her. Blankets?

"Alejandro," she breathed, knowing even in sleep who had moved her. She reached for him, wound her arms around his neck. "You are here," she said. "With me."

"Why were you on the chaise, Rebecca? It cannot be comfortable for the whole night."

"Bed's too big." She yawned.

"You have to sleep in the bed. It is better for you."

"Stay with me."

Did he groan? "I cannot," he said, gently pulling her arms away from his neck.

She was waking up by degrees, her mind becoming more alert. Alejandro was here, now. She'd been so lonely without him. Was it wrong of her to want him? To want to feel needed by him, even if only for a short while?

"Why don't you want me?" she asked, unable to keep the hurt from her voice.

"I don't want to hurt you."

He sat on the edge of the bed. She reached out, trailed her fingertips along his jaw. She could see him in the dim light from the moon—the hard lines of his face, the outline of his big body silhouetted against the pale wall behind him.

"You've already hurt me," she said softly. "What's one more time?"

"Go back to sleep, Rebecca." He kissed her palm and placed her hand over her heart.

She thought his hand ghosted over her hair, but she couldn't be sure.

CHAPTER ELEVEN

WHEN Alejandro told her they could marry while his sister was visiting, she didn't realize he meant that very afternoon. He'd presented her with a prenuptial agreement that morning. Somehow, after what she'd told him about her father and Parker, it hurt that he would shove a legal document at her that basically said he didn't trust her and ask her to sign it.

And, truthfully, it wasn't just about the agreement. She understood that a rich man—or woman—had to protect assets. But when she loved him so much, when she wanted him to love her in return, it simply drove home the fact this marriage was convenient, a means to an end. It was about the baby, not about her.

He'd watched her without speaking while she read it. It took a while, since her vision kept blurring.

"You do not wish your lawyers to see this first?" he'd asked, when she kept rereading the same clause.

"I can read a contract, Alejandro." And she could—but when this was about her life with the man she loved, about their future and their baby, it took longer to digest all the legalese. Finally she'd signed it, then excused herself. He'd let her go easily enough, and for that she was grateful.

Now, the four of them rode to the registry hall together. Valencia and her husband Philippe, who'd been able to get away from his business at the last minute, talked and laughed the entire way. Even Alejandro laughed from time to time. He clearly adored his sister. He was almost a different person with her around.

Rebecca could see why. Valencia's personality was infectious. She was a kind, happy person, and she loved her husband to distraction. Rebecca watched the other couple enviously. If Valencia loved her handsome Frenchman, then Philippe worshipped the ground his wife walked on. Their children, whom they'd left in France with his parents, were their pride and joy. It was a blessed existence they shared. Rebecca could only hope for a fraction of their happiness once her baby was born.

The ceremony was conducted in Spanish, with a translator for her—required by law—and was over quickly. Though she hadn't been in Spain the requisite amount of time to marry a citizen, Alejandro had somehow got around that detail. It was good to be rich and famous, apparently.

Valencia hugged her tight after it was over. "I am so glad my brother has you," she said in thick English. "You will make him happy. He deserves happiness, yes?"

Rebecca smiled tremulously. "Yes, he does."

Though he looked, to her, as if he'd be happier anywhere but standing in the registry office with a new bride. Fortunately his discomfort was not apparent to his sister or her husband. Philippe clapped him on the back and congratulated him profusely, and Valencia hugged him and whispered something in his ear.

After the wedding, they spent the afternoon shopping for baby furniture. Valencia was excited, Philippe marginally less so, but Alejandro wore a look of stony reserve. She imagined that shopping for baby things so soon, when they'd been married only a couple of hours and she didn't even look pregnant, was hard on him. He must surely be thinking of the last time he'd picked out cribs and bassinets.

She wanted to go to him, wanted to take his hand and squeeze it the way he'd squeezed hers when she had told him about Parker. Eventually, when they'd strolled into yet another store featuring yet more cribs, Rebecca found herself beside him. She put her hand into his and gave it a quick squeeze, before joining Valencia, who was cooing over sleepsuits and piling them into a basket.

By the time they arrived back at the villa after dinner, it was late. Valencia and Philippe retired to their room, and Rebecca decided to say good-night as well. Alejandro stopped her when she started up the stairs.

"We are in the master suite, *mi esposa*. It would be odd for us not to share a room now, *sí*?"

Blood thundering in her ears, she followed him to the room where they'd made love for the first time in five years. He stopped in the door and let her go through first. If she'd anticipated him carrying her over the threshold, she would have been disappointed. As expected, the memories assailed her as soon as she walked inside. She could see the bed in the room beyond the living area. Had she gotten pregnant there? Or had it happened in Dubai?

Fifteen minutes later, Alejandro still hadn't spoken. He showed no signs of heading into the bedroom any time soon. She remembered last night, how she'd so pitifully asked him to stay. How he'd refused. So now what?

Finally, she couldn't stand the silence any longer. "How are we to share a room together if you don't want to be in the same bed with me? Shall we play a game of tic-tac-toe to decide who gets the bed and who gets the couch? Or maybe you should just let me return to my own room."

He looked up from his seat on one of the leather couches flanking the television. He hadn't turned the TV on, had just sort of sunk wearily onto the leather with a glass of sherry and a dark look.

"The servants will talk, *querida*. Besides, I want to share a bed with you," he said. "Very much."

"But last night—"

"Last night we were not married." He spat the last word as if it were hemlock on his tongue.

She folded her arms and leaned against the arm of the opposite sofa, bemused. "Why did that matter? We've obviously spent the night together before." She pressed her hand to her stomach. "I have proof."

She tried to be lighthearted, but he didn't laugh. His gaze raked her from head to toe.

"You look tired," he said. "Why don't you get ready for bed?"

She slipped onto the cushion facing him. He was snappish because of the memories he'd had to endure today. "I'm sorry you had to go into all those stores. I know it must have been hard for you to look at baby things."

The black look on his face didn't change as he tossed back his drink. "I have a better idea," he said, rising to his feet. "Why don't we get ready for bed together?"

Before she knew what he planned, he was pushing her back on the couch, unbuttoning the cream silk dress she'd gotten married in, his lips following the gaping trail of buttons down between her breasts.

Sensation rocketed through her, so much more sweet and sensitive now that she was pregnant. She tried to concentrate, to focus on him. She knew what he was doing. Avoidance. Only this time he couldn't order her out of his sight. This time he had to shut her up with his mouth, his body.

Was it wrong to be happy about his methodology? Eagerly she went for his shirt, and he captured her mouth, thrusting his tongue inside to tangle with hers. He tasted like sherry, sweet and silky, and she shoved the shirt from his shoulders, her control slipping away with every caress, every breath.

"Alejandro, oh, I missed you…"

"I need you, Rebecca," he said seconds later.

Butterflies swarmed in her stomach as she kissed him again, fusing her mouth to his almost desperately. He'd never said that to her before. Not like that. *Want*, yes. *Need*, never.

He removed her dress while she shoved his trousers off. Underwear disappeared, and then there was nothing left between them but skin—damp, hot. She wrapped her legs around his waist as he rocked his hips against her. He stopped short of entering her body and she whimpered.

"I don't want to hurt you," he said, his eyes wildly searching hers.

"You won't. Make love to me. Please make love to me, Alejandro." Silently, she said the words she couldn't say: *I love you.*

Then he was thrusting deep inside her, their bodies rising to meet each other in perfect harmony.

Rebecca awoke sometime in the night, aware she was alone in bed. A light came from the living area. She searched for something to put on, found Alejandro's shirt. The tails went halfway down her thighs and she had to roll the sleeves several times. It smelled like him. She pulled the fabric over her nose, inhaled deeply.

Alejandro sat on the couch, a photo album on his lap. She stopped short, her heart thudding into her throat. But he looked up at her, and the movement prevented her from backing away, pretending she hadn't been there at all.

He didn't look angry. Emboldened, she went over and sat beside him, leaned her head against his shoulder. She didn't speak. Neither did he.

"She trusted me," he finally said. "I failed."

Rebecca climbed to her knees beside him, put her arms around him, leaned her head against his. "It's not your fault. It's no one's fault."

He didn't say anything.

"I went to tuck her in," he said a long while later. "She was blue. Her body was swollen with the fluids her heart couldn't pump. The doctors couldn't save her."

She stroked his hair. "I'm sorry."

"I cannot do it again."

"You won't have to." Her heart ached so much she thought it might burst.

"You do not know that," he said softly. "You cannot know it."

She took his hand, placed it over her abdomen. "I do," she said fiercely. "I won't let it happen."

"I have said the same thing," he replied. "But there are some things even I cannot control."

Something was wrong with him. He didn't feel right. He'd been on the edge of something for days now. Alejandro threw his pen down and swore violently. All he wanted to do was return home to the villa and make love to Rebecca. He should be over this compulsion by now, but it showed no signs of evaporating.

He'd told her about the night he'd found Anya. He'd never told anyone but the doctors. Never wanted to. He couldn't tell her, however, that he'd blamed *her* for the pain he'd suffered. It didn't seem right with her sitting there beside him, holding him, their baby growing inside her and her swearing she would not let the same thing happen again.

Did he still blame her? He couldn't be sure. One more thing that was wrong with him.

He'd had to force himself to come to the office today. He could work at home, but he'd gotten dressed and taken his Aston Martin Vanquish from the garage. Zipping through the streets of Madrid, he'd tried to concentrate on all he needed to accomplish.

It had worked for a little while, but now that he was at his desk his mind was wandering again. *Focus.* The hotel in Dubai was finally about to begin construction. Though it had been weeks since he'd uncovered his corporate spy, it had still taken time to disentangle the web and get everything straightened away with the Dubai authorities.

His reorganization of Layton International was proceeding. He always felt a little pang of guilt when he reviewed the progress. Absorbing the company had been a good move, but the difficulties he was experiencing with management made him long for the days when Rebecca had been in charge. She knew that company like she'd been born to it. He allowed himself a smile. Indeed, she *had* been born to it. Literally.

He'd considered more than once asking her to come back, but he couldn't sort out his feelings about it well enough to do so.

Was it a sign of defeat? Weakness? Was it tantamount to admitting he'd been wrong?

And what about the baby? Would work be too stressful on her pregnancy? Could she manage the hotel business and a baby too? A very male part of him wanted to lock her in the house and keep her there, but he knew from personal experience that whether or not a woman worked had nothing to do with her ability as a mother. Caridad had had nothing but time, and she'd failed miserably. His own mother was self-absorbed. Apparently so was Rebecca's.

He hadn't missed the disappointment on her face when her mother had finally called. The conversation had been short, to the point, and over without Rebecca saying more than a dozen words. Valencia had chattered endlessly to him about his marriage—she'd whispered that she liked Rebecca very much—though he could have done without it. He thought women liked to talk about those things. It seemed as if Rebecca and her mother did not.

Madre de Dios, he was married. If someone had told him

two months ago that not only would Rebecca Layton be pregnant with his child she would also be his wife, he would have never have believed it. Life was very strange sometimes.

His secretary came in with some paperwork, and he turned his attention to accomplishing something today other than thinking about his wife. Several hours later, when he'd spoken with his man in Dubai, negotiated a new contract in Russia and approved an impact study for a proposed site in India, he felt he'd done enough work to justify returning home. Perhaps Rebecca would be wearing that little bikini he'd bought her. She'd protested that she'd soon be too fat for it, but he'd bought it anyway.

There was nothing sexier than his wife lying beside the pool in her hot-pink bikini. Especially when she then let him take her into the house and peel it from her body as he kissed his way over every centimeter of her satiny skin.

He phoned down to the valet to have his car brought around. When he stepped outside to climb into the sleek gray car, reporters were waiting for him. He didn't think too much of it at first. Long after his years in the ring were over, the newspapers still seemed to find his life fascinating. Now that he'd so recently married they tended to shadow his and Rebecca's public appearances. The attention would die down soon enough.

"Señor Ramirez, is it true you systematically destroyed Layton International through an untraceable chain of subsidiaries? That you duped Jackson Layton into the acquisitions that led him into debt and contributed to his apparent suicide last year?"

Alejandro felt as if someone had kicked the ground out from under him. One minute he was standing firmly in place; the next he was searching for a foothold. "I acquired Layton International legally," he stated evenly, though he was seething inside. "You may check all the filings for your answer."

"But you owned the only bank that would lend him money. Was that a sound financial decision? Or calculation on your part? What does Rebecca Layton think about these revelations?"

"You mean Rebecca Ramirez," Alejandro said, in a voice very like a growl. Oh, he knew *exactly* what Rebecca thought. Exactly the lengths she would go to in order to do him harm. How had he ever thought she might be falling in love with him? Everything she did, every caress and kiss and sweet sigh, was nothing more than a lie.

She wanted to embarrass him, wanted his reputation to be damaged and his business interests to suffer. Did she think he would be forced to part with Layton International? That she would be waiting to snap it up? Did she think she could possibly win this battle?

"No more questions," Alejandro barked, before getting into the open door the valet held. He gunned the powerful engine and raced out onto the *paseo*. Traffic was heavy, but he barely noticed.

He was going to enjoy this confrontation. He'd been so close to falling off the precipice, to caring for her once more. Thank God she'd shown her hand. Finally everything made sense to him again. He had a purpose, a driving goal, a reason to lock her up and throw away the key. And when the baby was born he would be cutting his treacherous wife from both their lives.

"Thank you for the tea, Señora Flores," Rebecca said. The other woman smiled and dipped her head in a nod before retreating to the kitchen. Rebecca couldn't help but grin. She had been convinced, when she had first arrived, that Señora Flores hated her. Now the woman took pains to pamper her.

She sat at a table on the terrace, beneath the bougainvillea, and studied the fat book that the decorator Alejandro hired had compiled. She'd wanted to paint the baby's room herself— wanted to order fabrics and toys and pick out her own rocking chair. Alejandro had insisted it would be easier with a professional's help. But the woman he'd sent understood Rebecca's urges and had made a book with many samples to choose from. She'd also recommended combinations that went well together.

It was, Rebecca thought with a sigh, far easier than her plan had been.

"What would you like, my baby?" she said, flipping pages. "White wicker? Mahogany? Oak? Will we need pink or blue?"

They would not know the sex for many weeks yet, though she was secretly hoping for a girl. Little girls' clothes were so cute. And, since Rebecca was new at this mother thing, she figured she would understand a little girl better than a little boy. Perhaps the next one would be a boy.

A boy with Alejandro's smile.

A movement in the doorway caught her eye and she looked up. "Alejandro!" she exclaimed, jumping up just a little too excitedly. Damn, did she have to be so transparent? Surely the man knew she adored him, in spite of her best intentions not to give away the secret?

He looked stormy. Stony. Furious. Her steps faltered. "What's wrong, Alejandro? Did something happen at work? Is everything okay?"

He took two strides toward her, gripped her upper arms and glared down at her. "Is something wrong at work? You know very well something is wrong!" he thundered. "*Dios*, how did I ever fall for this act of yours again?"

He thrust her away and she wrapped her arms around herself, stared at him in shock. She could still feel the imprint of his fingers, the pain of his grip. Her stomach lodged somewhere in the vicinity of her toes. Her heart was sinking like a lead weight. Her limbs refused to move. *Oh, God.*

Even the birds had stopped singing. Señora Flores appeared in the doorway, disappeared again. Or it might not have been her. Rebecca wasn't sure because everything was blurry.

Breathe.

She had to get a grip on herself, had to control her emotions for the baby. "Tell me," she said very calmly. "I want to hear it from your lips."

He raked a hand through his hair, spun back to her. "As if you don't know."

"Tell me!" she screamed, suddenly angry and—and *offended*! That was the word she wanted. *Offended.* How dared he?

His nostrils flared, his chest rising and falling hard. As if he'd run all the way here. As if he'd scaled a mountain to get to her. No doubt he had. An evil, ugly mountain of his own design.

"Do not get worked up," he ordered. "Think of the baby."

She dashed tears from her cheeks. "Or kittens and puppies. Anything but the nastiness in your mind."

"You went to the press," he said, stalking closer again. Whirling away. "You told them your father committed suicide and that it was *my fault*! You want to ruin me, Rebecca. You want Layton International back by any means necessary, *sí*? Well, you will not get it!" he roared. "I will *destroy* it first."

"Suicide?" She could only stare at him as she tried to process it. "What are you talking about? It was a single-engine plane crash. There was a pilot."

"Do not pretend you don't know! You are the one who told them this! You tried to make it look like I did something illegal—like I am a criminal. Just a lowly bullfighter who dared to aim too high, right?" He stopped his pacing and glared at her. "This, combined with the Dubai accusations, will make my shareholders think twice, yes? Ramirez

Enterprises is in for a rocky quarter, thanks to you. But it will not work! You will *not* win!"

Rebecca sucked in a breath, surprised it wasn't shaky or short. Strong emotion buffeted her, threatened her, but she held steady. She would not panic over this. Over him. Not ever again.

"So this is what you think of me." It was a statement, not a question. "You're more worried about a dip in stock prices than you are about me or our baby."

"No, *you* are more concerned with getting your precious company back. You are selfish, Rebecca. Selfish and manipulative. You planned this all along. You didn't take your pills, you got pregnant on purpose, and you faked a panic attack to get me to marry you!"

Icy calm wafted over her, chilled her down to the bone. Inside, her heart bled. Outside, she was detached. So cold it frightened her. She could see with such clarity now. She'd been right about him. The man she loved was controlled by the angry, grief-stricken, suspicious man before her now. She loved him too, but she could not live with him.

"Then why did you marry me if you didn't want to?" she demanded. "No one held a gun to your head. We could have worked out visitation, if you wanted it."

"Visitation? This is *my* child."

"Are you sure?" As soon as she said it, she regretted it. The raw pain on his face told her she'd stabbed deep. But she was furious, hurt, and she wanted to hurt back.

His face was dark. "If not for the timing, I might doubt it."

She swallowed a bubble of hysteria. "Because I am a slut, of course. I'll sleep with anyone for advantage, right? My God, you make me sick." After everything she'd told him, everything she'd felt and believed. It was too much to process. She didn't even bother gathering up the sample book. She just headed for the door.

"Where are you going?"

"Away from you."

"You cannot hide from the truth, *mi esposa*," he said nastily.

She turned back to him. He was a big blur in her field of vision. She swiped her tears away, shook her head. "But you can, can't you? You do it quite well."

CHAPTER TWELVE

ALEJANDRO did not feel any better. In fact he felt worse. After his confrontation with Rebecca he'd thought he would feel exhilaration, triumph, all the things he usually felt when he'd won a fight. Like he could conquer anything.

He *always* felt like he was bursting with life and energy when he won.

But not this time.

He sat in his study and blinked at the computer screen. Señora Flores brought him the drink he'd requested, dropping it on the desk with a thud and marching away without bothering to wipe up the splashes that had landed on the mahogany. She was angry with him for yelling at Rebecca.

He focused on the news headlines he'd been reading. It was there—the sensational story about Jackson Layton's suicide and Alejandro's part in pushing the man over the brink. He'd had all his phones diverted to an answering service hours ago. Reporters would be calling nonstop. Hell, there were probably a few camped outside his gates.

Rebecca had accused him of hiding from the truth. The charge stung, though he knew she was wrong. Why did her barbs prick at him when *she* was the one who had lied and cheated?

He put his head in his hands, stared at the wood grain, the

way a drop of moisture was beginning to stain the surface. Odd how just that little drop could change the wood—the color bleaching out, the grain showing clearer, the visible blotch on what had once been a perfect surface.

What if he was wrong? What if the perfect surface of what he'd thought was true had a blemish? Why would she wait weeks to feed this story to the press?

He thought back over the last few weeks—thought of everything he knew about her. Nothing she had done, if he truly examined it from all angles, showed calculation. Someone with an agenda would have had a better plan. Did it make sense to get pregnant on purpose, but then leave the instant she learned he'd owned the bank and resorts? Wouldn't a woman with a plan to get her company back pretend not to know what he'd done? And wouldn't she plant misleading stories to the press far earlier?

Anyone could have brought this story out now to try and discredit him. Someone with a grudge over the Dubai contracts, in fact. Cahill? He'd been the one to send Rebecca documents, and he'd be just crafty enough to hold a story until it would do him the most good.

Alejandro sat there for a long time, not touching the drink, not moving. Just thinking.

Finally, he lifted his head. *"Maldito sea."*

He shoved himself to his feet, sought her out. But every room he went into was empty. His heart began to pound a drumbeat in his chest, growing faster with each successive room.

Señora Flores met him in the foyer when he came full circle. She did not look happy to see him. "Señora Ramirez, she has gone."

The best thing about being Señora Ramirez was that she could walk into the Villa de Musica, demand a room for the night, and no one would blink. She knew Alejandro would track her down eventually, but at least she'd have a few hours' peace.

Not surprisingly, the room the staff put her in was the suite, with all its memories. Just her luck.

She'd cried a bucketload earlier, but she was startlingly out of tears now. She couldn't even muster a whimper. She went into the bedroom they'd once shared and sank into a chair by the window. Below, traffic was moving steadily. Across the street, a man and woman argued. She could tell because she could see their arms waving back and forth. And then they were kissing.

If only her problems were solved so easily.

She would ask for a divorce. There was no other way. She would not live with him—not as cold and unforgiving and suspicious as he was. If he wouldn't divorce her, she'd insist on her own place. A house nearby, or an apartment. They would live separately, but they would parent their child together.

And how is that going to work, Rebecca?

She pushed a hand through her hair. She didn't know, and she didn't have the energy to think about it right now. She just sat and stared and planned random scenarios, none of them truly viable.

Her respite didn't last long. An hour, maybe two, and then she heard the chime announcing someone had entered the room.

"Rebecca."

She didn't even glance at the entry. She'd felt his presence before he'd spoken. The soft, sexy timbre of his voice stroked her abused senses. She was far too weak with this man.

"I want a divorce, Alejandro."

"No."

She bolted up from the chair, faced him across the room, her arms rigid at her sides. She'd never felt more like doing battle in her life. "I will not stay married to you, living in that house, putting up with your abuse. You wouldn't know the truth if it fell on top of you, so don't you *dare* come in here with the idea you're going to force me to go back with you. Not tonight, Alejandro. Maybe not ever."

"*Sí*, I agree."

Her eyes narrowed as she watched him. He looked a little haggard, as if he'd been working hard and hadn't had enough rest. He wore khakis and a dark button-down shirt, and he looked so delicious she wanted to press her mouth to the hollow of his throat and taste the saltiness of his skin.

Folding her arms beneath her breasts, she turned her head away. "You agree to a divorce? So quickly?"

"That is not what I said." He came into the room, shoved his hands in his pockets and went to the window. Close to her, but not too close. She would have to take at least three steps to be beside him.

"Then what are you saying? Because I'm too drained to figure it out."

"The truth, Rebecca. It has been staring me in the face."

She let out a heavy sigh. He wasn't making any sense.

"Will you sit?" he asked. "I want to say things."

"Fine." She went over and sat on the edge of the bed— away from him. He leaned against the windowsill, as if he realized she would not welcome him moving close again.

"I found Parker Gaines," he said softly. "I did it the night after you told me about him."

Her heart suddenly felt like it was beating in a sea of molasses. "Okay," she said, stupidly.

"He is in a California prison for embezzlement."

Was it wrong to feel satisfaction at the knowledge? "Good."

"Yes, I thought so as well. It saved me the trouble of killing him for you."

"Alejandro—"

"No," he said, holding up a hand to silence her. "I would do this gladly. You need only ask. When he gets out in twenty years I will challenge him to a duel."

In spite of herself, she grinned. Not much, but still a grin. She tilted her head down to hide it.

"Are you laughing at me, Rebecca?"

She wanted to, but she shook her head.

He sighed. "Ah, well, I am not so amusing."

He didn't say anything for so long she looked up to see what he was doing. He was staring back at her.

"I know you did not give the story to the press," he said gravely.

If he hoped that news would make her leap up and throw herself in his arms, he was mistaken. "And? Did you hire someone to tell you this? Find the real culprit so you could no longer blame me?"

"No, I did none of these things. I just know."

She did laugh this time—and it was as bitter as acid. "How can you suddenly just *know*? It's not like you, Alejandro! You've done something and you're lying to me about it."

He moved with a speed that startled her. When she would have scrambled away, he dropped to his knees in front of her, gripped her hands. "I know because of many things, *amor*. I know you are not capable of this kind of deception. It's too calculated, too cold—"

She tried to wrench her hands away, but he wouldn't let go. "But this is exactly what you've been accusing me of all along! I'm cold, calculating. I'll sleep with anyone for anything, I make bargains on my back and—"

"Stop," he ordered. "I was wrong."

She searched his eyes, looking for deceit. "I don't understand you," she whispered.

"Can you forgive me for the things I've said? The things I've done?"

"I don't know," she said honestly. She stared at their clenched hands. His dark ones gripping her paler ones. "You've hurt me too many times. I'm not sure I can take that risk again. Or that I want to."

He let her go and she pulled away, stood up and moved out of his reach, while he remained kneeling by the bed. He dropped his forehead on the edge of the mattress, stayed that way for several moments.

Her heart slammed her ribs at seeing him like that. She didn't understand it, didn't know why he would go to such lengths. Had she missed some sort of Spanish law about mothers getting full custody of children in divorces? About foreigners married to Spaniards for less than a month? Did he need her to come back so he could take their baby away?

She pressed a hand to her abdomen protectively.

"I blamed you," he said. "That's why I did it."

"What?"

He looked up. "For Anya. I blamed you."

Horror coated her in iciness. "That makes no sense, Alejandro. How could it be *my* fault?"

He got to his feet, began to pace. "My father arranged for my brother to marry the daughter of one of his friends—a man he owed money to. When my brother died, my father wished me to honor the agreement. I have told you this, *sí*?"

She nodded, not quite sure where he was going with this.

"But I did not want to marry her. I wanted to choose my own wife, in my own time. So I refused. And then you ran because you thought I was engaged. I tried to explain this to you, but you did not believe me. Nor did I believe that you ever really loved me once Cahill pulled my deal. So I agreed to marry Caridad. She had all the right qualifications: bloodline, wealth, beauty. It was a marriage of convenience, and I was satisfied. She would be the perfect wife for me."

He blew out a breath, raked his hand through his hair. "I

was wrong. When Anya was born Caridad didn't seem to care. She was always distant and cold. This did not bother me until she was the same with our child. I knew I had made a mistake."

He stopped and faced her. "The night Anya died, Caridad was in Milan. She was unreachable for many hours. And when I did track her down she refused to come home until the next afternoon, because there was nothing she could do for Anya."

Rebecca's heart squeezed. She wanted to wrap her arms around him, but she was frozen in place. "And you blamed *me* for this? Why?"

"I chose to marry her because you left me, Rebecca. Everything that happened to me and to Anya happened because you left."

Resentment and sorrow mingled, burned deep. Her throat hurt as she forced the words to come. "You had a choice, Alejandro. There is always a choice. Just like my father had when he chose to pursue the Thailand acquisition. It is not your fault he was there, or that he got on that plane. He made his own choice. Just as you did. And had you *not* married Caridad you would have never had the joy of Anya. You wouldn't have suffered the pain, but you wouldn't have had the beauty either."

"I know this now. You have made me see it. You have made me see many things about myself I do not like," he finished quietly.

"Why are you saying this to me now? How do I know you won't blame me for something else, or accuse me of betraying you again?" She shook her head. "I don't want to take a chance and have it blow up in my face."

He drew in a sharp breath, let it out in a rush. "*Dios*, I must learn to let go, yes? You said the world will still move without me forcing it, so I have to take this leap. With you, Rebecca. I cannot do it alone."

Her lungs felt tight, but it wasn't panic closing in on her. Did she dare to hope? Or was he simply saying he would try better at their marriage? "Tell me what you mean, Alejandro. You have to say the words so I can be sure I understand you clearly."

"I am saying I wanted to marry *you* five years ago, Rebecca. I cared for you. It has taken me much thinking to realize the truth. And the truth is that I would not have been so angry you left had I not loved you."

Tears pricked her eyes. "You're saying you loved me when we were together before?" She could scarcely believe it. It was what she'd wanted then, more than anything. To be loved in return by the only man she had ever lost her heart to. But did he truly mean it? Could they get past all the hurt and anger between them?

"I loved you then. I love you now." He closed his eyes and bowed his head. "I am terrified of this love."

She knew why. "Because you don't have power over it." For him, the loss of control would be devastating.

"*Sí,*" he replied, suddenly looking at her with such tenderness she thought her knees would buckle if she weren't already sitting down.

"I'm not sure what to say, Alejandro." But her pulse was racing and her body was humming with energy.

"Say you love me too."

She couldn't deny it. She had no wish to. "I never stopped."

"*Madre de Dios, gracias,*" he offered skyward. "Does this mean you will forgive me?"

"I'm working on it. I need time."

He looked disappointed, but resigned. "You will tell me when?"

She nodded. She thought he might leave her alone now, but he shoved his hands into his pockets and turned to look out the window. She didn't know how long they stayed like that—

him looking outside, her sitting in the chair, thinking about everything that had happened. She wanted to believe him. She wanted to go to him.

And yet—

Each time she'd opened herself to him in the past she'd been hurt. She looked at his profile, his proud features, and realized just how hard this had been for him. To tell her everything, to admit he was wrong, to declare he loved her. If he could take that chance, couldn't she?

Rebecca got up, and he turned at the movement. She went and wrapped her arms around his neck and he caught her close, buried his face in her hair. They stayed that way for several minutes, not talking, just holding each other. Finally she pushed him back just a little, so she could look at his gorgeous face. Yes, it was a leap, but she had to do it with him. She had to trust him with her heart and soul.

"I think I forgive you now. I love you, Alejandro. I always have."

He kissed her so sweetly she could have cried. *"Mi corazón,"* he whispered. "You have enslaved me. I fought you but I did not win."

"Are you sorry?"

His smile lit up her world. "There are no losers in this game, *mi amor*. I am, finally, your willing slave."

She gave him a wicked smile as she reached for his belt. "I can think of a few commands for my slave."

"I had hoped you would say so," he said fervently.

Life, Rebecca decided, was about to get a whole lot more interesting.

EPILOGUE

REBECCA emerged from the limo after her doctor's appointment and headed into Ramirez Enterprises. The appointment had been simply routine now she was closer to her due date. The genetic testing had revealed months ago that their baby would not be at any higher risk than was usual.

The receptionist greeted her with a smile as she strode into the lobby. She stepped into the private elevator and let the operator send her to Alejandro's office. The business was as strong as ever. Once Rebecca had united with Alejandro for a joint statement to the press about her father, the speculation had died down and the rumor had disappeared.

Further, when Alejandro had announced she was joining Ramirez Enterprises as the lead consultant to the hotel division, share prices had taken off. And she had no qualms about charging him an exorbitant fee for her expertise, husband or not.

Alejandro looked up from his desk. "I thought you were working from home today, *mi amor*?"

She shrugged. "I have already completed the projections for your next big project. Besides, I wanted to see you."

One eyebrow lifted. "Dare I hope why?"

"You may hope."

He came around the desk and pulled her gently into his embrace. "I can hardly get my arms around you."

"Alejandro, no woman likes to be called fat. Shame on you."

He laughed. "You aren't fat, *mi amor*. You are radiant."

She lost herself in his kiss. A second later, he seated her in a cushy chair. He put his hands on either side of her, tilting her back. "So tell me," he said, his lips ghosting over hers, down her neck, back up again. "What did the doctor say?"

"Veronica is perfectly healthy. I too am healthy as a horse. And just about as big." Rebecca frowned. How the man still found her attractive, she would never know.

"Yes, but can we still make love so close to your due date?"

"You really want to?"

He took her hand, pressed it to his groin. "What do you think?"

Rebecca sucked in a breath. *Oh, my…* "I think you need glasses."

"I think I adore you. I need you, *mi amor*."

"It would be cruel of me to deny you."

"Oh, indeed."

"Lock the door."

"Consider it done."

When he returned, he pulled her with him to the leather sofa and took her in his arms again. He gazed into her face with a look so serious it took her breath away. "You have made my life more wonderful than I ever thought possible. I am truly blessed."

"Alejandro," she breathed, "you are my everything."

And then she proved it to him.

A month later, Veronica Rebecca Angelica Rivera de Ramirez made her long-awaited debut—much to the delight of her parents. Eight months after that Rebecca was pregnant again—with twins. Life in the Ramirez household was never boring, but it *was* filled with love and laughter—and a few kittens and puppies.

* * * * *

Turn the page for an exclusive extract from
THE PRINCE'S CAPTIVE WIFE
by
Marion Lennox

Bedded and wedded—by blackmail!

Nine years ago Prince Andreas Karedes left Australia to inherit his royal duties, but unbeknownst to him he left a woman pregnant.

Innocent young Holly tragically lost their baby and remained on her parents' farm to be near her tiny son's final resting place, wishing Andreas would return!

A royal scandal is about to break: a dirt-digging journalist has discovered Holly's secret, so Andreas forces his childhood sweetheart to come and face him! Passion runs high as Andreas issues an ultimatum: to avoid scandal, Holly must become his royal bride!

"She was only seventeen?"

"We're talking ten years ago. I was barely out of my teens myself."

"Does that make a difference?" The uncrowned king of Aristo stared across his massive desk at his younger brother, his aquiline face dark with fury. "Have we not had enough scandal?"

"Not of my making." Prince Andreas Christos Karedes, third in line to the Crown of Aristo, stood his ground against his older brother with the disdain he always used in this family of testosterone-driven males. His father and brothers might be acknowledged womanizers, but Andreas made sure his affairs were discreet.

"Until now," Sebastian said. "Not counting your singularly spectacular divorce, which had a massive impact. But this is worse. You will have to sort it before it explodes over all of us."

"How the hell can I sort it?"

"Get rid of her."

"You're not saying…"

"Kill her?" Sebastian smiled up at his younger brother, obviously rejecting the idea—though a tinge of regret in his voice said the option wasn't altogether unattractive.

And Andreas even sympathized. Since their father's

death, all three brothers had been dragged through the mire of the media spotlight, and the political unrest was threatening to destroy them. In their thirties, impossibly handsome, wealthy beyond belief, indulged and feted, the brothers were now facing realities they had no idea what to do with.

"Though if I was our father…" Sebastian added, and Andreas shuddered. Who knew what the old king would have done if he'd discovered Holly's secret? Thank God he'd never found out. Not that King Aegeus could have taken the moral high ground. It was, after all, his father's past actions that had gotten them into this mess.

"You'll make a better king than our father ever was," Andreas said softly. "What filthy dealing made him dispose of the royal diamond?"

"That's my concern," Sebastian said. There could be no royal coronation until the diamond was found—they all knew that—but the way the media was baying for blood there might not be a coronation even then. Without the diamond the rules had changed. If any more scandals broke… "This girl…"

"Holly."

"You remember her?"

"Of course I remember her."

"Then she'll be easy to find. We'll buy her off—do whatever it takes, but she mustn't talk to anyone."

"If she wanted to make a scandal she could have done it years ago."

"So it's been simmering in the wings for years. To have it surface now…" Sebastian rose and fixed Andreas with a look that was almost as deadly as the one used by the old king. "It can't happen, brother. We have to make sure she's not in a position to bring us down."

"I'll contact her."

"You'll go nowhere near her until we're sure of her

reaction. Not even a phone call, brother. For all we know her phones are already tapped. I'll have her brought here."

"I can arrange…"

"You stay right out of it until she's on our soil. You're heading the corruption inquiry. With Alex on his honeymoon with Maria—of all the times for him to demand to marry, this must surely be the worst—I need you more than ever. If you leave now and this leaks, we can almost guarantee losing the crown."

"So how do you propose to persuade her to come?"

"Oh, I'll persuade her," Sebastian said grimly. "She's only a slip of a girl. She might be your past, but there's no way she's messing with our future."

* * * * *

Be sure to look for
THE PRINCE'S CAPTIVE WIFE
by Marion Lennox,
available September 2009
from Harlequin Presents®!

TWO CROWNS, TWO ISLANDS, ONE LEGACY

A royal family, torn apart by pride and its lust for power, reunited by purity and passion

Pick up the next adventures in this passionate series!

THE PRINCE'S CAPTIVE WIFE
by Marion Lennox, September 2009

THE SHEIKH'S FORBIDDEN VIRGIN
by Kate Hewitt, October 2009

THE GREEK BILLIONAIRE'S INNOCENT PRINCESS
by Chantelle Shaw, November 2009

THE FUTURE KING'S LOVE-CHILD
by Melanie Milburne, December 2009

RUTHLESS BOSS, ROYAL MISTRESS
by Natalie Anderson, January 2010

THE DESERT KING'S HOUSEKEEPER BRIDE
by Carol Marinelli, February 2010

HARLEQUIN *Presents*

International Billionaires

Life is a game of power and pleasure.
And these men play to win!

THE VIRGIN SECRETARY'S IMPOSSIBLE BOSS
by **Carole Mortimer**

Billionaire Linus loves a challenge.
During one snowbound Scottish night
the temperature rises with his sensible
personal assistant. With sparks flying,
how can Andi resist?

Book #2854

Available September 2009

HP12854

EXTRA

TAKEN: AT THE BOSS'S COMMAND

His every demand will *be met!*

Whether he's a British billionaire, an Argentinian polo player, an Italian tycoon or a Greek magnate, these men demand the very best of everything—and everyone....

Working with him is one thing—marrying him is *quite* another. But when the boss chooses his bride, there's no option but to say I do!

Catch all the heart-racing stories, available September 2009:

The Boss's Inexperienced Secretary #69

by HELEN BROOKS

Argentinian Playboy, Unexpected Love-Child #70

by CHANTELLE SHAW

The Tuscan Tycoon's Pregnant Housekeeper #71

by CHRISTINA HOLLIS

Kept by Her Greek Boss #72

by KATHRYN ROSS

www.eHarlequin.com

HPE0909

REQUEST YOUR FREE BOOKS!

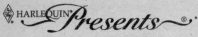 HARLEQUIN *Presents*

2 FREE NOVELS PLUS 2 FREE GIFTS!

PASSION GUARANTEED SEDUCTION

YES! Please send me 2 FREE Harlequin Presents® novels and my 2 FREE gifts (gifts are worth about $10). After receiving them, if I don't wish to receive any more books, I can return the shipping statement marked "cancel". If I don't cancel, I will receive 6 brand-new novels every month and be billed just $4.05 per book in the U.S. or $4.74 per book in Canada. That's a savings of close to 15% off the cover price! It's quite a bargain! Shipping and handling is just 50¢ per book*. I understand that accepting the 2 free books and gifts places me under no obligation to buy anything. I can always return a shipment and cancel at any time. Even if I never buy another book, the two free books and gifts are mine to keep forever.   106 HDN EYRQ 306 HDN EYR2

Name _____ (PLEASE PRINT) _____

Address _____ Apt. # _____

City _____ State/Prov. _____ Zip/Postal Code _____

Signature (if under 18, a parent or guardian must sign) _____

Mail to the **Harlequin Reader Service:**
IN U.S.A.: P.O. Box 1867, Buffalo, NY 14240-1867
IN CANADA: P.O. Box 609, Fort Erie, Ontario L2A 5X3

Not valid to current subscribers of Harlequin Presents books.

Are you a current subscriber of Harlequin Presents books and want to receive the larger-print edition? Call 1-800-873-8635 today!

* Terms and prices subject to change without notice. Prices do not include applicable taxes. Sales tax applicable in N.Y. Canadian residents will be charged applicable provincial taxes and GST. Offer not valid in Quebec. This offer is limited to one order per household. All orders subject to approval. Credit or debit balances in a customer's account(s) may be offset by any other outstanding balance owed by or to the customer. Please allow 4 to 6 weeks for delivery. Offer available while quantities last.

Your Privacy: Harlequin Books is committed to protecting your privacy. Our Privacy Policy is available online at www.eHarlequin.com or upon request from the Reader Service. From time to time we make our lists of customers available to reputable third parties who may have a product or service of interest to you. If you would prefer we not share your name and address, please check here. ☐

HP09R